ROGUE ROYAL

MEGAN SLAYER

Rogue Royal
ISBN # 978-1-83943-750-2
©Copyright Megan Slayer 2021
Cover Art by Kelly Martin ©Copyright November 2021
Interior text design by Claire Siemaszkiewicz
Pride Publishing

Anthologies
Aim High: Lifetime Hitch
Brothers in Arms: One Night with You
Rules of Summer: Summer Stock

Collections
What's his Passion?: Wild Card
Love's Bloom: Love Next Door
Sun, Sea and…: Sun, Sea and Summer Songs

ROGUE ROYAL

Dedication

For the Lucky Ducks
For my editor because you make my work shine.
♥

Chapter One

"I'm in charge." Charlie stared out at the kingdom, admiring the park leading to the hall of government. Snow lay soft on the ground and the land looked crisp but clean. The trees were dusted in bright white and kids played on the grounds of the park, tossing snowballs at one another.

He'd used to toss snowballs—before his father had handed him the keys to the monarchy. He'd become the king. The entirety of Lysianna was now under his protection. He should feel invincible, but he didn't. To be honest, he didn't feel like a king.

He was just a man with a fancy crown...and an entire country expecting him to keep order.

"Sire? You have a problem?" Newt, one of the pages, held a document out. "Lord Spencer gave this to me. He's just finishing up in the other room. According to this, you must be married by end of this year. It's already December fifth."

"You're kidding me." He wanted to see Spencer right away. Why would his right-hand man send the page in to alert him to this notice? "I thought I had a while." He'd known about the time limit, but could've sworn the deadline was more than thirty days away.

Spencer swept into the room and flicked his fingers to dismiss Newt. "Go." He waited until Newt left the room, then continued. "You have to be married by the new year. That's how that rotten woman had the decree worded. You've had all year to pick, and now if you don't choose, the kingdom goes to the next in line."

"That's Zara's little boy, Alistair." He'd never know why she'd named her child that, but whatever. "Well, shit."

"What's worse? You're supposed to marry a girl. According to this, you need to procreate." Spencer shook his head. "You'd really think your former stepmother hated your guts."

"She did." He leaned back in his office chair. "She wanted nothing more than to ruin my life." His former stepmother had sworn that he and his sister Zara weren't right for the crown. She'd wanted to be queen, and when the king had stepped down, she'd lost her connection to the line. She hated her stepchildren and even more that Charlie was gay. Unfortunately, she'd managed to get a decree into the records which stated that Charlie, the current king, needed to not only be married, but to have children.

"What are you going to do?" Spencer asked.

"Nothing yet." He had no prospects or ideas—just a kingdom to himself. He wasn't good at being alone. Ever since he'd come out, he'd had a boyfriend. Being with someone made him feel more secure. Except now... He didn't know what to do.

"We should throw a ball." Spencer clasped his hands behind his back. "That's it. A ball to find you a...husband. Would he be the prince? We don't have co-kings. Duke? That doesn't feel right."

"It doesn't matter, since I don't have anyone in mind," Charlie said. "Plan out the ball. I don't care. I've got roughly thirty days to find a husband. It's only almost impossible."

"I'm on it." Spencer picked up his tablet. "We'll have to fast-track the details, but it's been done before."

"A king should be self-assured, not wallowing in self-pity. So I'm alone and being forced to wed?" He stared at Spencer. "I'm the king, right? So I can add an addendum to the decree, correct? Saying that I'm entitled to marry the man I choose, not a woman, since I'm gay?"

"You can. I'll get the decree written up." Spencer took his place at his desk. "Won't be more than a minute to get the words on the parchment."

Charlie paced the length of the office. He had no business being king. Sure, he could handle passing judgments and thought himself fair, but he wanted to be happy — not just there to mete out justice.

He wanted to be loved in the way Zara had found love with Luke. They were meant for each other and the stuff of fairy tales.

What about him? It'd taken most of the year for the people of the empire to warm up to him being gay and the king. Would they accept him being married to another man? For all he knew, they'd revolt.

Spencer finished writing up the document. "Here. Look this over and sign it if the wording is correct. This addendum should at least give you the right to marry a man. But I should mention, you've always been roguish in the way you handle things. This isn't that far out of normalcy for you. Don't sweat it."

"Thanks." He settled behind his desk and read through the document. If he needed something done fast and correctly, then Spencer was his man.

"So, we'll have the ball on the twenty-fourth." Spencer held his tablet again. "You'll find someone among the attendees, but this gives us a small pad in case you can't."

"I suppose." He signed the document. He should take the reins on the ball and his search for a husband. "For the ball, I want the colors blue and silver. Not Christmas colors. Everyone should attend wearing blue or silver. Advertise it as a Christmas event, not my misadventures in finding a possible husband."

Spencer nodded. "Understood, but I would brace yourself. Once the pages find out there will be a ball, the speculation will run rampant. Everyone knows you need to find a husband and they'll try to figure out who it will be."

"Of course." He knew the staff liked to gossip. "I don't like the idea of this forced marriage. It's unfair."

"Not if you find a good husband — and you could." Spencer continued, tapping on his tablet. "It's a long shot, but it's possible."

"How? I don't have time to meet anyone. I'm busy with affairs of state." Charlie stared out the window. "How will I know that the man I've met at the ball will be the right one? After one night? It's ludicrous. For all I know, the guy is just trying to get money from the family."

"I know," Spencer said. "I'm glad your father divorced your former stepmother, because all she wanted was to see you fail. She was determined to have the Earl of Lender take over as king. Now, because of her, he believes he's owed the position."

"I know." He wasn't a fan of Lender. People who wanted something for nothing drove him berserk. Lender had married to get his title, bought his position in government, paid off individuals to keep from getting sued after he left office disgraced and had still managed to con the former queen into helping him attempt to gain a position in the line of succession. Lender didn't belong there. Charlie sighed again. "Here's to hoping that I find someone before we get to the point where Lender thinks he's got a chance."

"Agreed." Spencer stopped tapping. "You need to go to the solarium now. It's almost time for the interview with *Media Magazine*. They want to take your photo first, but they wanted something informal."

"They don't want me walking around in the snow? I assumed they'd want me to be strolling through the park or something." The magazine had a certain look for their photos and most included formality.

"No, they want you to look relaxed." Spencer tucked the tablet to his chest. "They want to discuss you being on the throne."

"It's boring." He snorted. "What else do I say? It's thrilling?" He left his seat and gestured to the door. "Let's go." He made his way through the castle to the solarium at the west end of the building. The camera crew had already set up the shot and the brunette interviewer stood next to the oversized carved chair. Her pantsuit swathing her body in crimson, she drummed her fingers on the back of the chair.

Charlie sighed. He didn't mind the publicity aspect of his role, but he hated answering the same questions over and over. Besides that, everyone wanted to know about his sister. *So why not ask her to sit for the interview?* She was quite approachable and happy now that she'd married Luke, had Alistair and settled into life as a mother.

Spencer directed Charlie to the main chair. "They insisted you sit here. Not the throne."

"Why?"

"It looks royal," Spencer replied.

He rolled his eyes, then pasted a smile on his lips. "Very well."

"King Charles." The interviewer gasped, then bowed. "It's a pleasure to meet you. I'm Lady Teresa Eushe and I'm humbled to be in your presence."

"I'm honored you've chosen me for the interview. You didn't need to set up such a posh space. I'm a simple man." He nodded to her. "Shall we?"

"Yes." She gestured to the fancy chair. "First, let's get the photos, then we can chat."

"Of course." He'd done a dozen of these interviews. Every magazine and paper wanted a report on his 'hot bachelor king status'. He didn't see the big deal. He didn't have a significant other because the right one hadn't come along. That didn't mean he couldn't rule. It just meant he wasn't getting any.

He suffered through the interview and expected the woman to bring up his string of ex-boyfriends. Until his father had stepped down as king, Charlie hadn't expected to become the leader so soon. He'd thought he had time to play the field and find a husband properly.

He listened to the woman chatter, but the view out of the windows caught his attention. A man and a little boy were walking along the brick path leading past the solarium. Charlie wondered who the man was and why they hadn't met before. He knew the little boy—

Heather Dawn's son, Emmett. The child wasn't the best at reading and Charlie recalled being told the boy needed tutoring to get up to his grade level. Was this man the tutor? Or Heather Dawn's new boyfriend? She had two young boys and Charlie couldn't imagine being a parent.

The man, though, caught Charlie's attention. The coat covered his frame, but he appeared trim and Charlie liked the way the slight winter breeze caught in his dark hair. He had a thing for dark, brooding and handsome men. Was this one brooding?

"Do you believe you'll find a husband before the deadline?" Lady Teresa asked. "Are you aware Lender believes he's next in line to the throne?"

Shit. He needed to pay attention and not watch the guy outside. "I'm confident I'll find someone, although I believe this decree to be out of date. A ruler should be permitted to choose a worthy partner on his or her own timeframe."

"And Lender?" she asked.

"Has no connections to the crown. He's not in line." Not if he had anything to say about it.

Spencer nodded behind her. "Is that your last question? The king is very busy and needs to attend to the planning of the Christmas Ball."

"One more," she said. "What would you like to tell our readers and your loyal subjects? Any words of wisdom?"

"Yes, I appreciate every one of my subjects and I'm endeavoring to do what's best for all of them. We are a proud nation and should be proud to be of the kingdom of Lysianna. I am both humble and proud to be your leader and hope to be for many years to come." God, he needed to work on his speaking skills.

"Thank you." She stood and shook hands with him. "It's a pleasure to have interviewed you. So easy."

"You're welcome here any time. Thank you for interviewing me." He stood and watched the team pick up the gear. At least she hadn't begged him to pose in his crown.

He waited until the crew and interviewer had left, then settled on the chair again. "Spence? Anything else? I need a break."

Spencer checked the tablet. "You have a meeting with the planning commission for the Christmas festivities. They wish to show you the itinerary for the royal celebrations and will want to incorporate the ball into their plans. They've got in mind a rather large bash for the New Year portion of the celebrations."

"Of course." He folded his arms and looked out of the window again. "Who is the guy with Emmett? Is he new?"

"Him?" Spencer rubbed his chin. "That's Nathan Pratt. He works as a tutor and with archives. Seems bright and fair. I'm not sure if he's gay, but I was told he'd used a surrogate to have his son. The surrogate is one of your subjects, so since the child is half-Lysiannan, Nathan was permitted to live here as he raised the boy." He eyed Charlie. "Do you wish to meet him?"

"Maybe." He wasn't sure if he wanted to make a move. Still, Nathan was handsome in a faraway manner. He must be decent enough with kids if he had one. But would he be dazzled by Charlie's role as the king and not genuine?

One of the stewards brought in coffee and snacks.

"Thank you," Charlie said and smiled. "How are you, Cort?"

The steward blushed before he blushed. "I'm well, your highness."

Charlie clasped his hands together. Cort couldn't be more than eighteen and looked every bit the young man he had to be. "I have a question. Are you happy here?" He knew Cort's name, but not much else about him. "To be working for the crown?"

"Will I get sent to the gallows if I answer wrong?" The color drained from Cort's face. "I'm not supposed to talk to you, am I? And this is a test?"

"You may speak to me," Charlie said. "I enjoy your company. Feel free to talk to me whenever you like."

"Wow." Cort stood tall and clasped his hands together. "You're nicer than I was told."

"Who told you I'm mean? No one will die if you're honest." Charlie picked up the cup of coffee. "Tell me."

"Cook. She said you're grumpy."

"Only at five in the morning." He laughed. "Thank you for your honesty and the coffee. I'll return the cups later. You're dismissed."

"Yes, my king." Cort tripped over his feet as he left the room.

"Nice kid." Charlie leaned on the chair. "So young and impressionable."

"They get younger every day," Spencer said. "He's a bit young for you."

"Spence? Seriously?" He crinkled his nose. "I'd like someone closer to my age. Are there any men, late-twenties or early thirties, single and looking to be with a man who wants love, tenderness and a partner? Find that for me and we'll talk."

"It gives me a better idea as to what to look for." Spencer abandoned the tablet on the tray. "Do you want to meet Nathan?"

"He's got a kid?" Charlie asked. "I wouldn't turn down someone who happened to be a father."

"You're kidding." Spencer snorted. "What about who will inherit the throne?"

"It'll be Alistair. That's already been arranged." He didn't see the big deal. "Look, I haven't found anyone yet and we still have to plan the gala or ball—that the interviewer already knew about. I thought we'd just decided on it."

"I let her know while you were getting your picture taken." Spencer shrugged. "It's going to come out sooner than later."

"True," Charlie said. "Focus on the ball."

"Very good," Spencer replied. "I'll be right back."

Charlie sank onto the carved chair and sighed. What Spencer didn't understand was that he wanted to find someone. He didn't want to be lonely, but he needed to find the right person.

He gazed out of the window at Nathan. He had no idea if they'd be compatible or if Nathan would even want to date a king. He might not even be gay. The unknowns didn't mean Charlie couldn't gawk at him and consider what could be.

He was a king and deserved a fairy-tale ending, right?

Chapter Two

Nathan walked Emmett back to the school building and waved as Emmett headed in. He liked Emmett and, given a little more time, the child would be reading at his grade level. Emmett was a bright student, but tended to transpose letters. Nathan had told Heather Dawn to take the boy to the pediatrician for a proper diagnosis, but it sure seemed the child had dyslexia. There would be a better plan for how to help Emmett after the consultation with the doctor.

Nathan checked his watch after the boy had disappeared into the building. He had half an hour to get to his job in the archives. If he hurried, he'd get to see his son, River, for a few minutes along the way.

At six months old, River still slept a lot, but was more active when he was awake. He'd mastered sitting up and was already eating cereal with mashed bananas. Nathan just wanted him to grow up healthy and wished he could spend more time with the child. He missed out on so many of River's milestones, like when he'd rolled over for the first time.

He jogged across the grounds to the apartment he kept. If he'd worked things right, he'd be there as River was having his meal. He hurried up to the second floor to change his clothes. Mrs. Major was sitting on one of the kitchen chairs and feeding River.

"Hi," she said. "You're on time."

"I rushed." He ruffled River's thin hair. "I wanted to see him for a few minutes."

"I think he's happy you did." She cleaned cereal off River's chin as the child giggled. "Better step back if you don't want to wear it. He's a messy eater."

"I don't mind." He'd rather be the one feeding his son, but he had to get to the archives in twenty or so minutes. "I wanted to grab a sweater. The archives are chilly already, but in this snowy weather, it's worse. I swear they have a draft."

"It's possible. The archives are supposed to be state of the art, but it is cold out." She fed River another spoonful of the gloopy cereal. "Be grateful you're not in the oldest part of the castle. I know that's drafty."

He ducked into the bedroom to retrieve the sweater, then returned to the kitchen. "I forget how much I miss being with River until I have to dart off to one of my jobs."

"It's natural." She cleaned River's chin again. "Mack called. He wanted to know if you were home."

"And?" Nathan asked. "What else did he want?"

"To be nosy." She fed River another spoonful of cereal. "He didn't ask about River or how you were doing. I had to give scant info."

"Typical. Mack is self-centered. He probably forgot River existed. He never wanted to be a father," Nathan said. "Did he want anything?"

"Just to know if you were home. I told him you were busy in the other room." She shrugged. "I'm not going to tell him you're working two jobs to keep body and soul together. That's not his business."

"Thanks." She'd handled the situation well. Better than he'd have done.

"He said that's good, and when I asked if he wanted to speak to you, he declined. No message either." She frowned. "I'm sorry."

"It's fine." Not really, but he had little choice. Nathan had been the one to want a child. He'd found the surrogate and done the work to get the ball rolling. Six months into the process and before River had been born, Mack had broken things off. When asked why, Mack had claimed he never wanted kids and couldn't be with a father. Instead of worrying at home about Mack, Nathan had opted to live in Lysianna with his son. He liked the small country. It was quaint and no one seemed to care that he was a gay single father.

"Nathan?"

He snapped to attention. "Shit. Sorry."

"You'll be late." She smiled and nodded to the door. "Give him a kiss and get moving. The faster you get to work, the faster you can come home. He's been staying awake until half past eight, so if you hurry, he'll still be up."

"Thanks." He'd been given a gift when he met Mrs. Major. She'd become the nanny and friend he needed. She came over whenever he requested and didn't complain—plus, she'd become a mother figure to him, too.

"See you at eight," she said. "Go."

"Yes." He'd be on time today. He'd get his work done and not become engrossed in the old manuscripts.

He kissed River on the head and tousled his downy hair. "See you, munchkin."

"Good luck." Mrs. Major waved as he left the apartment.

Nathan hustled to the ground floor and over toward the archives building. Along the way, he gazed at the solarium portion of the castle. He loved the glasswork in the room and the wrought iron along the foundation. The craftsmen who'd built the portion of the building had taken extra care to ensure its iron forms looked organic rather than geometric.

He spotted a man in the solarium. *The king?* He'd never met the king and wouldn't know him if he saw him.

Whoever he was, he seemed sad. Cute, but sad. Like someone had stressed him out. Nathan wondered who he was and what had him upset. Tingles shot through his body as he looked at the man. He couldn't remember the last time he'd felt this way. Probably before Mack. He longed to go into the solarium and talk to the sad guy.

Maybe he could lift the man's spirits.

Nathan left the path and crossed over to the solarium door. He expected guards or something by the doors, but maybe this wasn't an exclusive area or the king wasn't around. He opened the door and stepped into the solarium. "Hi."

"Hi." The man looked up. "May I help you? Are you lost?"

"No, I work in the archives. I'm piecing together a manuscript from the seventeenth century. It's a book of love poems." He wasn't sure why he'd shared that bit of information. "I saw you here and you looked so sad. Did the king chew you out?"

"No." The man smiled. "He hasn't."

"Why do you look so upset? Do you need to speak to the king? I'm told he's not so bad — not that I've met him." Nathan shrugged to hide his slight fear and concern that he'd overstepped his boundaries. "Is there something I can do?"

When he walked over to the man and looked into his eyes, a spark shot through Nathan's system. He could stare at this guy forever.

"You've already helped me," the man said.

"I did?"

"You cheered me up. I've had a lot on my mind and will be seeing royalty, so you talking to me has helped settle my nerves." The man smiled again. "Who is my archivist in a shimmery blue coat?"

"It's royal blue." Why did he have to sound so dorky? "My name is Nathan Pratt." He held out his hand. "It's nice to meet you."

"I'm honored to meet you, Nathan." He shook hands with him.

Sparks skittered along his skin and Nathan could've sworn time slowed to a crawl. "And you are?" He should ask, right?

"Charlie." He held on to Nathan's hand for another moment before letting go. "I needed a smile, and you've done that. Thank you. Do you always make people smile?"

"I try," Nathan said. He'd like to hold hands with Charlie again. "When you meet with the royals, I hope they go easy on you, Charlie. I should get moving. I'm due at the archives at five and it's probably past that now."

"I wouldn't worry about it," Charlie said. "You've done me a great service. It's like you knew I needed someone."

"It's a gift." He hesitated. He didn't want this moment to end. "Do you want to get coffee some time?" It was a bold move, asking Charlie out, but if he didn't try, he'd never know. Charlie made him want to be bold.

"I'd like that." Charlie's smile increased in wattage. "That'd be nice."

Such white teeth, and what a goofy smile. Charlie's eyes glittered. Nathan fiddled with his sweater hem. God, he was thirty-two years old and tugging on his sweater as a nervous gesture. "I should go."

"Don't you want my number to text me to get together?" Charlie wriggled his fingers. "Here, I'll put it in for you."

"Oh. Yeah." *Duh.* He handed over his phone. "I'll text you later."

Charlie added his digits. "I'd like that."

"I'm going." God, he was late, but he wanted to keep talking to Charlie. He'd also like to sound intelligent with his responses.

"You should."

"Like now." He had to get his feet moving. "I'll see you."

"Right." Charlie tucked his hands into his pockets. "Later."

"Yes." This was getting awkward, but he wasn't sure what else to say. "I— Bye." He escaped the solarium and welcomed the chilly December air to quell the fever in his veins. He needed a moment to catch his breath, too. Something about Charlie demanded his attention, yet seemed so normal.

He wondered why Charlie had to meet with the royals. He should've asked, but maybe it wasn't his business. Maybe he'd ask later.

He hurried to the archives and into the foyer. The secretary waved as he rushed past. He'd be in so much trouble. It was already past five and he should've clocked in right at the top of the hour.

He removed his sweater and stopped at his desk to switch into his lab coat, then grabbed his gloves.

"Where were you?" Leroy, the head of the archives, stormed up to Nathan. "You're late. Again."

"I know. I stopped to see someone in the castle." Nathan donned his gloves. "I'm sorry."

"Then it is true." Leroy's eyes widened. "I'm sorry. I'll leave you to your work."

"Okay." He didn't understand. "Is everything all right? How many more times can I be late before I'm discharged?" He needed to know. He didn't plan on being late again, but anything was possible.

"Don't worry about it." Leroy left Nathan's desk. "Good luck."

"Yeah." He touched Leroy's arm. "Why are you acting strange? Normally, you'd have ripped into me."

Leroy frowned, then chuckled. "You don't know?"

"No, I don't. Did I speak to someone I shouldn't have?" He didn't understand. "What's wrong?"

"If you don't know, then it's probably better. Just be happy you're not in trouble for being late. Trust me." Leroy patted him on the shoulder. "It's all good."

He still didn't know what to make of what was happening, but he'd have to ask Charlie if he'd done something wrong. Maybe Charlie knew the inside scoop on who to avoid.

Nathan threw himself into organizing the folio of manuscript pages. The papers themselves were in decent shape, but had been placed haphazardly in the folio. The information in the pages wasn't interesting, but some of the manuscripts weren't that exciting. Still, he loved his job archiving and working on the documents.

He moved the first five pages out of the way, then picked through the other documents to find the next pages. The corners of the papers would need some restoration, but that could be done once the thing was in order.

An hour later, he'd managed to piece the entire manuscript together and labeled the folio for the restoration crew.

Aymee, one of the secretaries, rushed up to him. "You have a letter." She nudged him. "Nathan, you have a royal invitation. You'll take me with you, please? I never get to attend the palace events."

"What?" He accepted the heavy envelope. "What is this?" He looked at his name, carefully written in script on the front. If the item wasn't from the royal family, it sure looked important. "This is probably my firing letter."

"You're not being fired. The court just announced there will be a ball on Christmas Eve to celebrate the holiday and the king. It's exclusive, but everyone wants to be there. You have to have an invite to get in, and you do." She massaged his shoulders. "And now I know someone who has an invite. Maybe I could go with you?"

"Right, because you actually like me that much." He refused to attend a ball with someone who only wanted him because he could do something for them—again.

"What if this isn't what you think and instead it's a bill or summons because I've done something wrong?"

She rolled her eyes and stopped touching him. "You don't act out. Besides, this came via royal courier."

"So?" He didn't see the big deal.

"The royal couriers don't just hand out bills or summons. They come out when there's something big—like the ball." She leaned on his desk. "Nathan, you're a handsome man. What if the king wants you to be there because he's seen you and thinks you're hot? What if he's looking for people to be part of his court?"

"You've got to be kidding me." He snorted. It was a bad habit, him making such a noise, but it was involuntary. "I'm not good enough to be asked to a ball and I'm not even a citizen. That might be a requirement. What if this is something telling me to stay away? It could be."

"You're thinking too hard about this." She drummed her fingers on his desk. "Well? What is it?"

He opened the envelope and withdrew the card inside. As he scanned the writing, he had to admit that she was right and this was indeed an invitation.

"So?" She nudged him. "Nathan?"

"I've been invited to the royal gala. Christmas Eve—which is roughly three weeks away." He didn't have a proper suit. Or did he need a tuxedo? *Crap*. He had no idea how to dress for royal balls.

"And you're going to bring me along?" She wriggled her eyebrows. "Please? Can I see the invitation? I've never seen one."

"Here. You can look for yourself." He handed her the card.

She touched the gold edge. "The only time I received something from the crown, it was to commemorate my working for the royal family in the archives for two years. This is way better." She caressed the paper. "The ball is being held on Christmas Eve and you can bring a plus one. Me? Please?"

"I don't even know if I'll attend. What if I don't have a babysitter? I can't show up with my son on my hip. I'd be thrown out, so I probably won't accept. Dads don't need to attend balls," Nathan said. "Sorry."

"Nathan, you can't be serious." She groaned. "This is from the king. You can't ignore this or him."

"I can if I don't have a babysitter. What do I do if Mrs. Major is invited? She won't be able to watch River if that's the case," he said. "Being a parent sometimes means you don't get to do what you want."

"Sucks to be you." She placed the invitation on the table. "If you decide not to go, then may I have the invitation?"

"Sure, but it says my name. You can't exactly pass for me."

"I know." She kissed his cheek. "I'll win you over sooner or later, and you'll realize you want to take me. They'll see I'm not hurting anything by coming with you and it'll be fine."

"You do realize I'm gay." He closed the folio. "We can be friends, but it's not going anywhere after that. As for the ball, that's on you."

"The cute ones are always gay." She sighed. "Oh well."

"Sorry to let you down." He heaved a breath of relief as she left. An invitation. He hadn't been with the court for that long, and wasn't he really not vital to the royal family? He wasn't important. He simply reorganized and handled old manuscripts. Nothing about him was special. He resumed working on the additional pages of the second manuscript. If he wasn't careful, he'd be here all night working instead of being home with his son.

The invitation didn't matter.

His son did.

Chapter Three

Charlie finished his paperwork for the night and checked his phone again. He shouldn't be so worried about the text, but he'd felt a connection to Nathan. The man was handsome and inviting. He wanted to touch him. Did Nathan feel the same way? Did he feel the spark?

"What are you doing?" Spencer ventured into Charlie's office. "I sent the invitations — even the special ones."

"Good." He sat back in his chair. "Did you ensure one went to Nathan? Did you check on him?"

"We did." Spencer sat across from him. "He's thirty-two years old, single, a father to an infant son and a good worker — even if he has a tendency to run late."

Charlie froze. "A father?" *Oh, God.* He wasn't sure he wanted to be a father, despite his declaration that he wasn't opposed to dating a single dad.

"Yes. He and his partner had a child with a surrogate who lives here in Lysianna. The partner left and Nathan decided to raise his son here. He's working as a tutor and in the archives. We ran his information when we admitted him into the country and when the process with the surrogate went through. He checks."

"But he's a father." Charlie couldn't wrap his head around the concept. He'd have an instant family — if things with Nathan even progressed that far.

"Yes. The little boy, River, is cute." Spencer shrugged.

"You don't like kids. Why would you say he's cute?" Charlie asked. "When your sister had her kids, you bristled."

"I did, but her kids are now nine and seven respectively and they're out of control." Spencer stared at him. "I made sure Nathan was given an invite and I wouldn't have done so if I thought he wasn't worthy. You're my boss and my king, but you're also my friend. I refuse to even potentially put you on a collision course with someone who isn't worthy."

"Thanks." Charlie tried to smile, but tensed. "Was I too forward in wanting him to be invited?" He hated carrying so much concern, despite his ability to worry himself into a tizzy.

"You're second-guessing me. Why?" Spencer tipped his head. "I wasn't kidding. I don't let you get close to people with ill intentions."

"I know, but he hasn't texted me."

"So? He could be with his kid." Spencer checked his watch. "Actually, he should be getting out of work right around now, so he could be clocking out or just getting home. By the way, he has a tendency to be late, so he might be overwhelmed and busy. It might have slipped his mind."

"Has he been reprimanded for his lateness? I helped him to be tardy today." He didn't want Nathan to be punished.

"No. I told the head of archives to forgive him by order of the crown. He means well and is trying to care for his son while working two jobs and doing it all on his own—save for his babysitter. He's juggling a lot."

"You've overstepped," Charlie said. "But I appreciate it. I see what Zara is going through with Alistair, and Luke helps her. Being a parent seems hard, so thank you for assisting him."

"You're welcome," Spencer said. "I saw you with him and you seemed happy. Happier than I've seen you in a long time."

"I am." He rolled the pen away from him on the desk. "He doesn't know who I am."

"He doesn't?"

"Nope."

"Wow. Really?"

"My face is everywhere, so either he's good at acting or he didn't recognize me. I'd think he has to know it was me, but he seemed so sincere in his actions. I doubt he'd have approached if he knew he was talking to the king." If Nathan liked him without knowing he was royalty, then there was a chance he and Nathan could have a future.

"Just be careful. We've been fooled before." Spencer stood. "And realize he might not text until tomorrow. It's possible he'll forget altogether. You know where he'll be, so you could surprise him and show up where he is."

"I could." If he made the situation look coincidental and watch Nathan in the wild first, he'd have a better idea of Nathan's true nature. "I like it."

"I try to come up with good ideas." Spencer grinned. "I'll let you know if he responds with an RSVP for the ball—if he doesn't tell you himself."

"I can only hope." Charlie pushed away from his desk and walked with Spencer across the room. "I'm rusty at dating."

"You were with Mark a long time." Spencer stayed beside him as he ventured into the corridor. "We all thought you'd found your potential soul mate."

"So had I." He still regretted splitting from Mark. His ex wasn't perfect, but had seemed to like him.

"He used you." Spencer fell into step with him. "He asked many people in the court, including me, for money. He said it was for you, but I knew better. He'd tell your father you needed land you never asked for and wanted money to buy things that weren't something you'd like...he thought he'd get stuff for nothing."

"I know. As much as he lied, I wasn't good at dating or seeing him for what he was—full of shit." He'd thought Mark would change but Mark had let him down.

"It happens. We think we've found the right one, but there's something within us that says this isn't what we deserve. We hear that voice, but can't quite let go." Spencer shrugged. "When you find the right one, you'll know."

"I hope you're correct."

Spencer stopped at the royal suite. "You've got your phone with you, so go get some rest. We'll talk in the morning about the rest of the details for the ball and what to do about Nathan. Until then, don't sweat it."

"Easier said than done."

"I know," Spencer said. "I hope he texts, you have a long, deep conversation and you get what you want."

"That's what I'd love to happen."

"Go to sleep or whatever." Spencer waved and left Charlie at the door to his suite. Once Charlie stepped into the cavernous space, he realized just how much he hated silence. The rooms were so big and empty. Too quiet.

Memories hit him. He'd grown up in this suite. He'd played with his toy cars on the patterns in the carpet and stacked blocks on the window seat. He'd practiced his French horn in the guest room and let Zara put makeup on him in their parents' bedroom. He touched the drapes. He'd mourned his mother in this room and witnessed his stepmother pushing her way into the king's life here, too.

His phone buzzed and he almost dropped the device while trying to retrieve it from his pocket.

The number wasn't one he didn't know, so not Nathan.

Zara.

He answered the call. "Hi." He sank onto the window seat. "What's up?"

"A ball?" she asked.

That was his sister. No 'hi, how are you?' No 'hello, big brother...' just her blunt question. Now that she'd found her spine and gumption, she spoke her mind and he loved her ability to be honest with him. "I'm lonely," he said. "But I'm fine and I'll live. You?"

She groaned. "Sorry. How are you?"

"I just told you," he said. "What's the issue with the royal family throwing a ball?"

"It's so beneath you."

"I'm not interested in husband shopping, but it happens and I've got to do something that's out of my character," he said. "If it weren't for that ridiculous decree, I'd look for a partner when it suits my schedule."

"You'll never look."

32

"It wouldn't feel so rushed," he said. "I've been looking for someone, for your information, but the right guy hasn't crossed my path—at least I don't think he has yet." Nathan could be a good one, but they hadn't talked for very long and Nathan didn't know the truth.

"You keep pretty busy."

"I'm expected to keep the country running. In my role as the king, my time isn't my own and I can't just go to a bar to meet someone. When I do meet people, it's usually not someone I want to date. Maybe I'm too picky," he said. He'd been accused of wanting too much from his partners and expecting high standards. "Maybe I do require a lot of people."

"You're being forced to marry someone so you don't lose the crown—the one that belongs to *our family*—so I doubt you're aiming too high. You're under duress," Zara said. "It's not fair."

He appreciated her perspective on the situation. Ever since Zara had been pushed toward marriage with the duke, a totally unsuitable man, she'd decided to go her own course, which was just as well. She'd always been a free thinker, even if she did try to toe the family line.

"What do you want to do?" she asked. "If given the choice, what is yours?"

"I don't want the decree in place, but it's a law I can't change. Father approved of it when he'd been convinced our stepmother had our best interests at heart. She wanted the duke to be king—not me. She never thought I was good enough."

"She was wrong and then she hooked up with Lender," Zara mumbled. "I can't forget him. The rat."

"That's putting it mildly." He'd never liked Lender and wouldn't marry him for the crown or any other reason.

"So? What do you want to do?"

He didn't have to think about it. "I want to find someone who gets me. Someone who is kind and sweet, but willing to go on an adventure. Someone who doesn't mind my quirks and isn't overwhelmed by my being a king. Jesus. I need someone who isn't going to con me or crumble when things get tough. Is that too much to ask?"

"It might be impossible," she said.

"It will." He harbored no doubts that he was in a world of trouble trying to find his perfect match.

"But there could be someone out there."

"How'd you know Luke was the one?" He'd never asked her that before.

"When he traveled here to Lysianna to be with me. That took guts, but it also took you. I can never make that up to you," Zara said. "It was a huge thing to do."

"He wanted to be with you, little girl. I just had to file the paperwork." He longed for a partner who'd sacrifice all to be with the person he loved.

"One day," she said. "I hope the ball doesn't work and you can find someone before it happens. That way it's not a marriage party, but rather a true celebration of your happiness."

He'd love for that to happen, too. "Let's not get ahead of ourselves." He yawned. "I should go. Thanks for giving me crap. I needed it."

"Always. I love you, Charlie."

"You, too, kid." He hung up and flopped onto the bed. He should get some rest. If Nathan was going to text, then he would, and there was no point in staring at the phone.

He left the bed, brushed his teeth, stripped and switched into a pair of sleep shorts, then collapsed into bed. He fell asleep in minutes. Until now, he hadn't realized how worn down he'd become in just a short period of time. He needed a few hours of not worrying about finding a husband and the affairs of state. His life stressed him out. What if no one wanted to try for the job of husband to the king? What if only sycophants or hangers-on wanted the position? What if someone wanted to use him?

He woke with a start and sat up in the pitch-black room. He gulped to catch his breath. *What time is it?* He glanced at the clock. *Four in the morning.*

Charlie scrubbed both hands over his face. He didn't need to get up for another couple hours and should try to get a little more sleep before starting his day. Right now, he needed to stop thinking about his love life and focus on his job as the king. The people needed him to be at his best and he wouldn't be without a few more hours of shut-eye.

* * * *

Charlie woke again at six-twenty and began his day. By two in the afternoon, he'd read through various documents and listened to three disputes between people in the kingdom. He didn't mind the politics of being the king, but he hated approving decorations and guest lists. He'd never been good at knowing what colors went together or if the swirls and sparkles were acceptable at the same time. If he had his way, everything would be dark blue and black with silver accents. Easy, simple and his favorite colors.

"We sent out the invitations." Charlie signed the last document. "Spence? What else do we have to do?"

"We did, and the first batch was for other royals and eligible bachelors in your social set," Spencer said. "But a king can marry a commoner, so this round involved the eligible bachelors of the kingdom."

He rolled his eyes. "Social sets, commoners…"

"I know." Spencer handed him a folder. "This is the music list and the menu."

He honestly didn't care. "Remember when finding a partner involved romance?"

"You're a king."

"So?"

"The decree?"

"I remember." How could he forget? Or be allowed to forget?

"It's not fair, but complaining about it won't change the fact that you've got to find someone." Spencer stood and cleared his throat. "You have a visitor. I tried to prevent him from getting in, but apparently he pushed through. Lender's here."

"Jesus." He wasn't in the mood to see the count. "Why?"

"Probably to check your progress. He's an evil-minded man." Spencer crinkled his nose. "Either he wants to see how you're doing with the marriage thing or he wants you to marry him and unite forces."

"I'd rather die."

"He'd arrange that." Spencer bowed his head and rushed to the door. "Count Earl of Lender."

The count strode into the room. He might have been ten years older than Charlie, but he looked far older than that and he wasn't Charlie's type at all. "My king."

"Earl." Charlie didn't like him or how he'd wormed his way into the line of succession. He'd be damned if he'd give Lender respect.

"Count," Lender corrected. "I see you're holding a ball. I wasn't invited."

Charlie had to measure his words carefully. "You weren't invited to ensure that if something happens, one of us will still be here to rule." It sounded diplomatic and awful.

"You're thinking of me?" Lender smiled. "How kind. You could abdicate and give me the throne. It would save you the hassle of finding a husband on such short notice and give you time to find what you want instead of scrambling. You're not going to find someone at the ball. There isn't enough time."

"Maybe not, but this is a kingdom and I *am* royalty," Charlie said. "Ever hear of fairy tales and them coming true?"

"This is reality," Lender snapped. "You don't belong in a leadership position if you're going to think in terms of fairy tales."

"You underestimate me."

"I know you're not ready."

Charlie shrugged to hide his outrage. "That's your opinion, not mine. Do you have business with me? Or are you here to chat?"

"I wanted to speak to you about the transition of power." Lender grinned. "You won't find someone, so we should plan for when I take over."

"You're addressing the king," Spencer said. "Remember your place."

"I know my place," Lender snarled. "And I know you won't have a place when I'm the king. You'll be removed from the kingdom in the first wave."

Charlie sighed. "Right now, your place is outside." He remained seated. "Go."

"Go? This will be my office soon enough," Lender snarled. "I should see what I'll be given."

"Not with that attitude." Charlie shuffled papers on his desk. "Guard?"

Two guards entered the room and grasped Lender by his arms. Lender stopped protesting. "When I'm the king, neither of you will be welcome on palace grounds or in this country. I will have you run out."

Charlie gestured to Spencer to shut the door. Once the room was secured, Charlie spoke. "He wants to drive me berserk and won't quit until he succeeds."

"You need to get married before he forces you out." Spencer folded his arms. "What do you want to do?"

"I want to see Nathan." He'd have a better chance of sparking something with Nathan than some random person at the ball.

"Did he text?"

"No."

"He might not."

"I know." He'd put a lot of faith into Nathan actually connecting with him.

"He could be busy. Remember, he's a father."

"I know."

"Give him some time. He could've been busy last night or forgotten all about texting. Maybe the baby got sick and he spent half the night up with him."

"Thanks." He needed that reality check. He pushed away from his desk and stood before the window. When the stress got to him, he hiked a few miles in the fresh air. "I'm going for a run. I need to get out of the castle for a while and stretch my legs. Want to come along? I'll have my GPS on and the detail follows me everywhere."

"I'll join you," Spencer said. "I don't trust Lender to leave you alone, so yes, I'm coming along. Meet you here in five?"

"Sure." He crossed the room to the adjoining changing room. It wouldn't take long to switch into his running gear. He'd have to stretch, but that wasn't hard. He tucked his phone into the secure pocket of his running pants, then carried his shoes with him back into the office.

Spencer arrived a moment later and sat with Charlie on the sofa while he put on and tied his shoes.

"You know, if people don't know you're a king, they wouldn't guess it." Spencer stood. "You're so low-key."

"I learned it from Zara." He tied his shoes, then stood. "Let's stretch."

"Why don't you act like a king?" Spencer sat on the floor and grasped his foot in the first stretch. "Honestly, you could command someone to marry you."

Charlie switched legs and continued his pre-run activities. "I could, but what's the romance in that? Honestly, if that's what I wanted to do, then I'd force you into marrying me, but you'd hate it and me. Plus, we're friends and I trust you more than almost anyone else. I don't want to ruin that."

"I would hate your guts."

"It wouldn't be fair, either."

"I guess not."

He stared at Spencer. "Be serious. Do you want to marry me?"

"Not really. I have a boyfriend and I like going home at the end of the night," Spencer said. "I doubt things with Ren are permanent, but it's nice to have someone that's not part of the royal family."

"See? You and I should be with someone we love and happy, not pushed." He bent over, touching his toes. "Besides, I don't want to lose you as a friend when you realize being married to me isn't much fun. You'd have to be a royal and you like your alone time. You'd never be out of the spotlight."

Spencer frowned. "I prefer to have a personal life."

"Well?" Part of him wouldn't mind being coupled up with Spencer, but the rest of him believed his assistant deserved better. He finished his battery of stretches.

"Nope." Spencer grinned. "You couldn't handle my messiness. I need the maid I've got just to clean up after me."

He swatted Spencer on the hip. "Let's go."

Spencer donned his earmuffs. "After you."

Charlie stepped onto the patio and tugged his gloves onto his hands. He set his music. Once he turned the app on to log his miles, he started off. He liked running with Spencer. There was no complaining or talking — just running. Spencer pushed him to go fast and not quit on himself. Plus, he didn't question the routes Charlie took. An hour later, he'd logged almost eight miles. His legs ached and his muscles screamed, but he didn't mind.

As he and Spencer hustled through the snowy park on the last quarter mile, Charlie spotted Nathan. He tapped Spencer's arm.

"Yeah?" Spencer shouted. He slowed his pace. "What?"

"I need a breather." He stopped his music and app, then nodded in Nathan's direction. "I'd like to talk to him."

Spencer yanked his earbuds free. "Who? Where?"

"Over there. Just stay close, okay?" His heart hammered. Part of him wanted to talk to Nathan and figure out what had gone wrong. The rest of him urged him to leave Nathan alone so he wouldn't be rejected.

What if Nathan had a good reason for not texting, like already having a boyfriend? "Hi."

Nathan looked up from his book and froze. "Hi." A half-smile formed on his lips. "How are you?"

"Good. You?"

Nathan swept his gaze over Charlie, then his lips parted. He didn't speak right away. "I'm hot," he said. "Oh God."

"What?" He must've heard Nathan wrong.

"You." Nathan waved his book. "In that...damn."

He'd forgotten he was wearing his running clothes—the form-fitting gear left little to the imagination. "Oh, this. I needed a run." If the sweat sliding down his temple wasn't evidence that he'd worked hard, he wasn't sure what would suffice.

"I saw," Nathan said. "You looked smooth. You've got a great stride."

"Do you run?" He hoped he did. He'd love another running partner.

"I did until River was born. He takes up most of my free time."

"River? Your son?"

"Yeah." Nathan tugged his phone out. "Here's his picture. He's rolling over now and chattering. He keeps me busy." He showed off the little boy. Thin hair on his head, chubby cheeks, bright blue eyes and drooly, but a cute child.

"I'll bet." Charlie bit back his sheepishness. A baby did require a lot of attention and he was selfish to demand some of Nathan's time.

"I meant to text you last night, but by the time I got River to bed, ate something myself and cleaned up, I'd forgotten all about you. Sounds terrible." Nathan shook his head and his cheeks darkened. "Having a kid sometimes kills romance."

Do I want a romance with Charlie? "You're busy." Charlie sat beside him and sucked in a ragged breath as the chill of the metal bench seeped through his clothes. *Damn.* When had the temperature dropped so fast? "Are you working tonight?" He bumped shoulders with Nathan. Sparks shot from his arm to his heart, then below his waistband. Now the temperature kicked up a few notches.

"I have to be at the archives at six. Why? I'd planned on going home to see River for a little while. Would you like to meet him? I'm sure my nanny, Mrs. Major, would like to meet you, too." Nathan folded his hands on his book.

"Sure. May I ask why you were sitting here in the park reading? It's a bit cold for such things. Why not go home and read where it's warm?" Charlie asked. "And yes, I'd love to meet your son and nanny."

"Oh this." He held up the book. "I'm reading ahead so I know what Emmett's working on and can help him better when I meet him during his reading time. I come out here because it's quiet, pleasant and no one bothers me. It's selfish, I suppose, but I can concentrate before I work with Emmett. He's a good kid, but he requires my focus."

"I'm sure." He'd never tried tutoring, but assumed it wasn't easy. "When do you have to return to the school?"

"I'm done with Emmett today, but I'll meet in ten minutes with his mother. If you'd like to come back at four, we can walk to my apartment together," Nathan said.

"I'd love to." He should tell Nathan who he was before things got any more complicated. Once Heather Dawn saw him, she'd tell Nathan the truth, and that wasn't how he wanted things to play out.

Nathan hopped up from the bench. "I need to go because I see her coming. See you in a little bit?"

"Sure. I'll be right back here once I change my clothes." He jogged away from Nathan before he crossed paths with Heather Dawn. Seconds later, he caught up to Spencer.

"Well? Why didn't he text?" Spencer fell into an easy jog beside him. "Is everyone okay?"

"His kid needed him." He jogged up to the private entrance to his quarters. "I guess the child takes up a lot of time — like with Zara and Alistair."

"And you buy that?"

"My father wasn't involved in my growing up, but that doesn't mean everyone goes that route. He seems involved and I find that attractive," Charlie said. "I'm meeting him and his kid at four."

"Charlie." Spencer stopped just inside the entrance. "Did you tell him who you are?"

"Not yet."

"Why?"

"If he likes me without the crown, then he should like me with it," he reasoned. "I want to know he's honest before I mention the royal title."

"Charlie." Spencer groaned. "I don't want this to backfire and I'm afraid it might. He seems nice, but he might not like being lied to — even if you have a good reason."

"I'll tell him at four," Charlie said. "I need to get changed. When I see him later, I'll mention it and see how things go. The fact he wants me to meet his son has to be a good sign." He kicked out of his running shoes, then rushed through the suite to the master bathroom.

"I'm not sure this will work, but I trust you," Spencer said. "I'll put the secret detail on you while you're meeting up with him, too."

Charlie nodded. He didn't have much time to get ready and this meeting was one of the most important of his life. "Deal."

Chapter Four

Nathan returned to the bench and waited for Charlie. He'd told him he'd be back in ten minutes, but the meeting had taken longer. He hated running behind, but couldn't help it this time. Would Charlie understand? Or even show? He shook his head. Charlie was a handsome man. Probably sought after, too. He'd never been good at dating or cruising for guys. He tended to be more reserved to the point of being timid.

"Hi." Charlie ambled up to him. "Are you done? I'm sorry I'm running behind. I had to speak to my friend, then shower, I hate meeting up with people and being sweaty from a run."

Nathan forgot what he wanted to say for a moment. Seeing Charlie stole his breath. The running garb before had accentuated the toned aspects of his physique and left nothing to the imagination. The sweater and jeans combination Charlie wore now looked so effortless on him. So perfect. Even the scarf appeared to be correctly paired with the outfit. Nathan had always wished he could be that put together, but half the time his socks didn't match.

"Nathan?" Charlie waved his hand in front of Nathan's face. "Are you okay?"

"You're fine," Nathan said. He'd love to run his tongue over every inch of Charlie's body. "Delicious."

"I'm what?" Charlie's eyebrows knotted, but he smiled. "Nathan?"

Oh, no. He'd verbalized his thoughts. *Crap.* He wasn't sure how to fix the situation. "Uh…"

"Are you okay?" Charlie asked. "You seem a little dazed."

"Just tired." Ah, his old standard answer.

"Being a dad and juggling two jobs must be difficult." Charlie sat beside him. "How do you manage?"

Now this he could answer. He stood and touched Charlie's arm. The zap shot straight to his brain, then his heart. *Oh God.* How was he supposed to think clearly when Charlie affected him on a molecular level? "Walk with me?"

"Sure." Charlie stood with him. "I admire you balancing everything. I don't know if I could."

"I have a great babysitter, but she likes being called a nanny. Mrs. Major is a life saver. She doesn't cost a ton of money and she's just about always willing to come over. If I didn't have her, I'd be sunk. Granted, it's not cheap to have her over most of the day. That's why I'm working two jobs."

"Makes sense." Charlie bumped shoulders with him. A smile curled on his lips.

Were the smile and touch intentional? Nathan wasn't sure, but he caught the whiff of Charlie's cologne—even that attracted him. He had to think straight and make conversation. "What do you do? You're not a parent, are you?"

"I'm in politics, which sometimes feels like I'm running a zoo or being a parent to a bunch of cranky people." Charlie shrugged. "I don't mind. I treat it like one big strategic style game."

"Are you good at it?" The question was probably silly, but he'd never known anyone in politics.

"I like to think so, but I'm not egotistical enough to know I am. I'm stuck in the job through December, so I'm trying to make the best of it," Charlie said.

"Does your job involve public functions and stuff?" He nodded to his building. "I'm on the second floor."

"I have to attend functions, yes." Charlie followed him into the foyer. "Do you like this place?"

"The price is right—I work for the royal family, so I get the apartment for free. Mrs. Major is across the hall, which helps. I guess her husband was a guard for the family. I never met him." He opened the door to his apartment. "This is me."

Mrs. Major sat on one of the kitchen chairs with River in his highchair as she fed him. She stood, then looked away. "Oh my."

Nathan ruffled River's hair. "Hi, little man." He smiled, then gestured to Charlie. "Mrs. Major, this is Charlie. Charlie, this is the famed Mrs. Major." He cleaned the cereal from River's face.

River giggled and pulled at Nathan's ear as he picked him up. "Daddy missed you," Nathan said and kissed his son. "This is Daddy's friend, Charlie."

Mrs. Major bowed before Charlie.

"What's going on?" Nathan asked. "What are you doing?"

"I should go." Mrs. Major stood. "I'll be back at six." She left without another word.

Strange. He'd never seen her that flighty. "Did I say something wrong?"

"It's me," Charlie said. "Hi, River."

"This is the one and only." He carried River over to Charlie. "This is my friend, Charlie."

River grasped the end of Charlie's scarf and tugged.

"Sorry. He's fast when he sees something he wants," Nathan said. "I used to wear a St. Christopher medal, but he ripped it off so many times, I gave up."

"Makes sense." Charlie stroked River's cheek. "My sister has a little boy, too."

"Yeah? How old?"

"Eight months." Charlie continued to touch River's cheek. "My brother-in-law is proud."

"He should be. Babies are hard to raise, but they're worth the effort." He gestured to the couch. "Sit? Do you want kids?"

"One day."

"That's the trouble, the guys want someday, but I'm a package deal." He had to put that out there. If Charlie wasn't interested in having kids, then they could be friends, but no more.

"Being a package deal isn't a bad problem to have." Charlie sat next to him. "May I hold him?"

"Sure." He allowed River to be held and River giggled as Charlie jostled him onto his lap. "He seems to like you," Nathan said. "He doesn't take to many people."

"It's a gift."

He spotted the invitation to the ball on his coffee table. He'd thought he put the correspondence away. "Did you get an invitation from the king to a ball?"

"Not yet." Charlie allowed River to stand on his lap. "You've got one, I see?"

"I did. I thought maybe everyone did, but if you didn't... You're a politician." He shrugged. "I don't know why I got invited. I don't know the king."

"Maybe it's so you can meet him." He held on to River's hands as the baby wobbled on his lap.

"Have you? Met him?" Nathan asked. "I haven't."

"That's what you said," Charlie replied. "I have."

"Then you should go to the ball. Maybe your invite is in the mail."

"Could be."

He stared at Charlie and admired his natural ability with River. Charlie was sexy in the parental role. Nathan wanted to make a move. The sparks between him and Charlie were off the charts and he looked forward to seeing Charlie. "If you could go to that ball, would you?"

"I would."

"Come with me." It wasn't a question. He shouldn't be so demanding. "I mean, would you come with me? I'd love it if you'd accompany me. It'd be nice to have a friendly face and someone to dance with. Plus, I kind of like you."

"Nathan."

The way he'd said Nathan's name brought Nathan down to Earth. He'd messed up. "Forget I asked. It's cool."

"Nathan." Charlie's shoulders sagged and he placed River on his lap.

"You know, I never asked if you were gay. For all I know, you've got a girlfriend." He left the sofa and paced. "I thought there was a connection and things were going well. You've got a knack with River and you seem to like me, too. I guess I read too much into it."

"They are going well."

He stopped with his back to Charlie. He needed to get a hold of himself and stop rushing. "Sorry."

"No need." Charlie held River and stood before Nathan. "I'm gay and I'm single. I don't have a girlfriend or beard. Oh, and the sparks are very real."

He'd felt them, too. *Thank God.* Plus, he looked so natural with River.

"They're real, but I need to be honest with you." Charlie cuddled River in his arms. "I'm not just a politician."

"Oh?" *He's married. He said he was single, but he's really married...* "What's the truth?"

"I didn't get invited to the ball because I'm throwing it."

"For the king, to curry favor?" That made more sense. "Okay."

"Sort of." Charlie toyed with River's small hand. "I'm the king."

"Of your political party." Sounded strange, but whatever. Maybe Lysianna called the head of the party the king. What did he know?

"No, I'm the actual king...as in the king of Lysianna." Charlie stared at him and said nothing else.

"Stop." He'd heard some crazy things in his time, but this was too much. "Just stop. You don't have to impress me, but you're freaking me out."

"I'm serious. I'm King Charles of Lysianna, the older brother of Princess Zara, otherwise known as Princess Catherine," Charlie said. "I'm giving the ball in order to find a husband, but I'd rather find someone in a more organic fashion—like how I met you."

"You're shitting me." He scooped River out of Charlie's arms. "I think you need to go."

"You don't understand. I never wanted to hurt you, but I wanted you to like me for me—not because I'm the king." Charlie's shoulders sagged. "I like you and I wanted this."

"You did?" The gall of this man... "Then you shouldn't have lied. I let you meet my son and I went out on a limb for you. I could've been arrested for going into the castle, but I thought you looked sad." He shook his head. "I can't believe I trusted you. Get out. I don't want go to your ball or see you ever again."

Charlie bowed his head. "Are you sure?"

"Yes." He shoved the invitation into Charlie's hands. "I don't even believe you're the king or that you're throwing it, but I don't care. I wouldn't go if I were paid to attend."

"I understand." Charlie clutched the invitation. "I do."

He held River tight. "Get out."

Charlie said nothing and left the apartment.

Once the door closed, tears blurred Nathan's vision. *A king? Right. Charlie could've come up with a better lie.*

River squirmed, then tugged at Nathan's collar.

"I trusted him." He willed the tears not to fall. "I thought he was different. Thought this thing happening between us was different. Yes, it was new, but I thought I found someone important for me."

He sank onto the couch and cuddled his son. His ex-boyfriend Mack had said he'd never find another good man. Wouldn't find someone who'd love him. He'd never be enough for someone. What did Mack know? Mack said Nathan trusted too easily. Believed in people too easily, too. Maybe he did.

Not with Charlie. The trust was gone.

The story was so far out there. A king! Why would Charlie lie about such things? Why impersonate a king when he could've been anyone else?

A knock on the door interrupted his depressed mood.

"Charlie, go away." He wasn't ready to argue with him right now.

"It's me," Mrs. Major said. "Nathan?"

"Come in." He wiped his cheeks and hoped she couldn't see he was upset. "Sorry."

She inched into the apartment. "What happened?" She shut the door. "Nathan? I saw the king leave and he looked upset."

"The king? Did he pay you to say that?" Nathan asked. "He is *not* the king. He's a guy who made up a story about being a king. Who lies about that stuff?"

She made her way across the room and scooped River from his arms. "You need to listen to me."

"Why? He's lying." He stood and paced the room again. "I've never seen the king, but I know he can't be him. He's young, handsome and out in public. Kings aren't meant to be young or visible."

"Nathan."

The softness of her voice stopped him in his tracks. He stared at her. "Mrs. Major?"

"When he showed up, I bowed to him because he *is* the king. Unlike his father, he strives to be visible and approachable. He tries to be informal, but that doesn't make him any less the king. I promise," she said. "He's a good man."

"It's not possible." *Can't be.*

"It doesn't seem that way, but it is," she said. "What did he tell you?"

"He said he's the king, but if it's true—which I doubt—then he's lied by omission." He shook his head. "It's ridiculous."

"Nathan." She tucked River into the crook of her arm and sat on the couch. "Sit. Please?"

Although he didn't want to, he complied.

"The king might not have told you the truth, but he did it because he's under the gun—so to speak. According to royal decree, he's got to find a husband in the next...not quite a month, I believe, or he loses the throne. I don't want to see that happen, because I like him. He's a fair king, but he's been cheated. People have lied to him. I'm guessing lots of individuals have tried to wiggle their way into the royal court because they want status or money. They want to be in line for the throne, too. Why not? They could be king or queen and that translates into him being used. I'm sure. He might not tell you, but we all have seen it. He met a guy who seemed wonderful, then it turned out that he wanted money. The guy tried to extort the family and it was all played out in public. I'm guessing the king is trying to protect himself."

"You're buying into this, too?" He groaned and shook his head. "You know the royal family, but this is so out there. I need to get showered for work and to think about anything except Charlie."

"I understand, but you're taking this the wrong way. He lied to protect himself, not to hurt you," she said. "I promise."

"Sure." He strode down the hallway to his bedroom and shut the door. He'd thought he'd found a good guy and they were at the start of a decent relationship. But the king situation...what Mrs. Major had said made sense, though.

He stared at his reflection in the mirror. It had to be the lighting, but he appeared older. He looked tired. Maybe it was the negative thoughts in his head or remembering the things that he'd heard, but he doubted a man who could be the king would be attracted to him. There wasn't anything exciting about him.

He splashed water on his face, then dried off. He couldn't solve his problems in the shower and couldn't talk to Charlie right now, either. *Crap.*

Nathan changed his clothes and combed his hair, then donned his glasses. He should get to the archives early and make up for his lost time the day before.

When he ventured out of the bedroom, Mrs. Major had River in her lap as she read a book to him. The baby slapped at the pages.

"Feel better?" she asked. "You look exhausted."

"I am." He gathered his things, then paused. "Why — if you knew he was the king — why didn't you tell me?"

"I never got the chance."

He hadn't given her the opportunity, true. "Would you have told me?"

"If you'd have asked, yes."

He sighed. "I'm sorry. I should've given you a chance to speak."

"It's all new." She smiled. "Are you heading out?"

"Yeah. I don't want to be late again." He kissed River on the forehead. "This way I can get home faster."

"Good. See you."

He waved, then left. His heart was heavy and his thoughts a mess. Could Charlie be the king? He seemed so down-to-earth. Nathan ventured out into the cold and tugged his jacket tighter around his body.

"Hi." A man sprinted up to him. "Are you Nathan Pratt?"

He tensed, but kept walking away from the apartment building. "Maybe."

"Were you with the king earlier today?" the man asked. "Walking together on a leisurely stroll?"

"No." Charlie wasn't the king.

"You weren't seen sharing a private moment on the bench in the park?"

"No." He was with Charlie, who wasn't the damn king.

"Funny. I've got photos of you together." He showed Nathan his phone. "See? I'm a reporter for the *Royal Rag*. It's a tabloid magazine, but don't let that bother you. I'm a damn good journalist."

"If you were so good, then you'd know it wasn't me." He looked at the image. It was so obvious it was him with Charlie.

"I see." The reporter nodded. "I won't be the only reporter to stop you. If you're seeing the king, then it's big news. He needs to get married or lose the crown. Watch your step."

Nathan shivered. He'd made a mistake in not only doubting Charlie, but also seeing him. He could be putting himself, but mostly River and Mrs. Major, in danger. He didn't want them bothered by the press. It wasn't fair.

What could he do? Beg Charlie for help after pushing him away? Charlie wouldn't give him the chance — not that he deserved it.

He should go home. He hustled across the park to the archives, then clocked in and out. His son needed him more than some old book.

As he doubled back across the park, another man approached him. This guy looked older than Nathan and not at all like a reporter. His clothes were too upscale. Nathan didn't know brands, but he could spot high-end materials a mile away. This guy knew how to dress well.

"Hi. May I have a word with you?" The man stepped into Nathan's path, blocking his way. "My name is Lender."

"Okay. So?" He needed to keep moving. "I'm late."

"This won't take more than a minute." Lender kept Nathan from walking away and got in Nathan's face. "I hear you're seeing the king."

"Who told you that?"

"Then you're not?"

"I don't know the king." Even if Charlie was the king, he wasn't about to admit it to this guy.

"Then you're not seeing him?" Lender grinned and put his arm around Nathan. "See, I don't want you to date him. I'd rather you run the other way."

"Why?" He hated the uncomfortable feeling. He swatted Lender's hand away as Lender stood beside him and squeezed his ass. "Stop. I don't know you and I don't like you at all."

"If you or anyone else gets involved with the king, you risk my gaining the throne. You don't want to keep me from my rightful place as king, do you?" He yanked Nathan close, as if they were a couple. "Don't mess this up for me. Leave the king alone. Got it?"

"And if I don't?" He debated his exit strategy. He was closer to the archives than the apartment building—good for security, but shitty for keeping his son safe.

"You don't want to risk your child's safety, do you? Don't want to put him in jeopardy, do you?" Lender asked.

"That's not fair." He wasn't interested in putting River or anyone else in danger.

"Oh no? It's not fair that I won't get the throne," Lender said. "I deserve it. Do you know how hard I had to kiss ass to get there? I had to pimp myself out to that witch. I deserve to be king."

You deserve to be ignored. "Okay." He wasn't about to put anyone in harm's way. Fuck that. "What do I need to do?"

"You let me handle things while you walk away from the king. Let him think you hate him and all will be well." Lender sneered at him. "Got it?"

"Yeah. I have business with the family because I work for the king, so I can't ignore him completely." *Fuck, fuck, fuck.* He had to see Charlie or the king or whatever, then get security tightened around his family.

"So? Soon, you'll be working for me. I'll ensure you get a raise." Lender grinned. "Might even put you in my inner circle."

"Sure. I need to get moving, though. I'm late." He pulled away from Lender. "Bye. I'll remember."

"Good." Lender remained in the park as Nathan walked away.

Nathan dashed into the archives. He couldn't use his phone, because he had no idea if he'd been not only followed, but bugged. Right now, he needed to call Charlie. If Charlie was indeed the king, then he'd be the one to help. This was bigger than one argument. "Aymee? I need to use the phone."

"Why?"

"I have a question on a royal document and I need to get authorization from the king's assistant." It sounded like a good enough lie to get through to Charlie. He reached over the desk and snagged the receiver from the cradle.

Aymee frowned. "Why didn't anyone tell me about this before now?"

"Because it just came up." He grasped the receiver. "Please?"

"I'll get you through," she said. "Anything else?"

"Yeah. I need to get word to Mrs. Major, my nanny, to bring River up here. Right now." His heart hammered. "I thought you'd like to see the baby."

"I would." She blushed. "You should be getting through. Where is your apartment? I'll go there myself."

"Hold on." He focused as the line clicked. "Hello?"

"The office of the king. This is Lord Spencer. How may I help you?"

"I need to speak to Charlie right now. I'm Nathan Pratt. It's about my son and my nanny and concerns Lender. Please?" Did he sound panicked? Lender scared him out of his wits. Could Lender be doing something already? Hell if he knew.

"Lender?" Spencer hesitated. "Just a moment." The line crackled. "He'll be right there." Once Spencer finished speaking, the line went dead.

Shit. He didn't want Charlie to show up, just to give him assistance. He couldn't help but be irritated with Charlie, despite wanting him.

Charlie thundered into the foyer. "What's going on? Where's Lender?"

"He threatened me." Nathan put the receiver back and his hands shook. "He said my son could be hurt if I didn't ignore you. I can't let that happen."

Spencer jogged into the room. "We've got the location secured and both individuals are on the way to the palace grounds."

Charlie nodded. "I wondered if he'd try something. I had my guards in place to execute this mission. Come on." He grabbed Nathan's hand.

Nathan wanted to argue, but saw no point. He wanted River to be safe more than he did to be angry with Charlie. Plus, he had no idea where they were going. He'd never been in the bowels of the palace.

Charlie took him into an office. Mrs. Major held a sobbing River. The moment Nathan saw his son, relief hit him hard. Tears streaked down his own face. "You're safe."

"We are." Mrs. Major hugged Nathan. "I hardly had time to think when the guards showed up. What's wrong? Did you upset the king?"

"Probably, but this isn't about that." He held River. "God. I thought…I don't know what I thought."

"Is this about the man who came to the apartment this morning?" Mrs. Major asked.

"What?" Nathan stared at her. "You never told me someone had come by."

"Tell me," Charlie said, butting into the conversation.

"A man came to the apartment and demanded to see River, but he didn't identify himself and didn't know River's name. Thankfully, River was in the playpen and out of sight. I gave up nothing and he left, but I also didn't answer the door until you came home. When I saw the king with you, I thought you knew about the visitor." Mrs. Major's hands trembled. "Who was he?"

Charlie held up a tablet. "Did he look like this, my good lady?"

Nathan shuddered. He'd never forget what Lender looked like.

"That's him." She grasped Charlie's arm. "Is that Lender? What does he want from Nathan and River?"

"To cause trouble." Charlie nodded to Spencer. "Go. I will not have this in my kingdom."

"Have what?" Nathan asked. He sank onto the chair. "Did you grab a bottle?" He doubted so, being that she and River had been escorted out.

"Can he have juice?" Charlie asked. "My sister's little boy is eight months and he's up to juice and just about anything else he can get his hands on. I have bottles of juice in my cupboard and mini-fridge."

Nathan's head swam. He'd heard what Charlie said, but he'd be damned if he could make sense of it now.

"I grabbed the diaper bag, but nothing else, and I forgot a bottle." Mrs. Major began to cry. "I'm sorry."

"Spencer is retrieving your things. Don't worry." Charlie withdrew a bottle from the cupboard and offered it to Nathan. "For the remainder of the month, I'm requiring you to stay here in the castle. I can't secure the apartment properly because there are too many variables around it, but I can here. You'll have the guest suite through the middle of January at least, and, Mrs. Major, I hope you'll stay with him. It'll ensure your safety. Plus, I owe you so much for your and your husband's loyalty to the crown, and for his sacrifices, as well."

"Thank you, my king," she said. "Thank you. I will."

Nathan gave the bottle to River. They were going to be moving again. *Damn it.* "Why does Lender want to hurt my family? You and I aren't together. We're not even sort of dating. We had a fight."

Charlie dropped to one knee at Nathan's feet. "First, you are my friend. We might have quarreled, but you're still my friend. Second, Lender is a bitter man who wants power and won't get it. Third, he thinks you're the one I've chosen to marry." He blushed. "And seeing how I'm kneeling, it does look questionable."

Nathan stared at Charlie. "You're kidding." He knew what he'd heard Charlie say and what Lender had growled about, but still.

"No."

One of the pages came into the room. "The suite is ready."

"Mrs. Major, if you'd like to go with Dustin, he'll get you settled in. Your things will be along by morning," Charlie said and stood.

"And the boys?" She gestured to Nathan and River. "They're my family, too."

"They'll be shortly behind. I wanted to speak to Nathan about the situation," Charlie said. "I hope you will feel safe here and know I'm endeavoring to get this matter handled as soon as possible."

"Yes, my king." She bowed, then followed Dustin from the room.

Nathan sighed. "What did you want to tell me? I'm an asshole for pushing you away, then demanding you help me? I already know."

"You can't be so informal with the king," Spencer snapped.

"Spence, it's fine. Please, leave me to speak to Mr. Pratt." Charlie shooed Spencer and everyone else from the room.

Nathan focused on giving River the bottle. He had his son in his arms and the rest of his problems didn't matter. He wasn't sure what he'd do next or how he'd work things out with Charlie, but that was a problem for another time.

Right now, he needed a moment to breathe—not think about how handsome Charlie looked, the way he smelled like sin or how he'd come through and saved the day...just like in a fairy tale.

Chapter Five

Charlie closed the office door. He needed to smooth over the situation and reassure Nathan. Plus, he wanted a chance to speak to him in private. The way they'd parted still rankled him. He didn't blame Nathan for being upset, but the problem with Lender was bigger than Nathan knew.

"Well, how do you feel? Are you okay?" Charlie asked.

"Me?" Nathan frowned, then plunked River on his lap, patting him to elicit a burp. "I'm shaky and freaked out. That man threatened my family."

"I know, and I'm sorry." Charlie dragged his chair over to where Nathan sat with River. "I can't imagine how you feel. I've never had my life threatened and I'm not a father. If it were my child being threatened, I'd be scared, too." If he and Nathan were parents to River, he'd move heaven and earth to keep them both safe. He liked Nathan and was enamored with River.

Nathan handed the empty bottle to Charlie. "Thank you. If it hadn't been for you, I'd be in the deep."

"I sort of got you into this." No, he'd dragged Nathan in over his head.

"You're really the king?" Nathan patted River's back until the child burped. "God, I don't even have a rag."

Charlie withdrew a handkerchief from his desk. "Use this."

"Thanks." He wiped River's mouth. "She's got the diaper bag. I feel so ill-equipped."

"It's okay." Charlie rested his elbows on his knees. "So, cards on the table?"

"Sure." Nathan bounced River on his knee and pressed his mouth to the top of the child's head.

"Cards on the table time. I am the king. Have been for just under a year. It's not easy, but it's interesting. I get to speak to all sorts of people and help everyone, but it's still politics. One of the downsides to my role is that I must be married to retain the crown. I believe I'm doing a decent job as the king and I'd like the chance to keep it going." He focused on Nathan. "That's why I'm throwing the ball on Christmas Eve."

"To keep your crown?"

"Yeah. The party is intended to help me find a husband." Saying the words out loud sounded awful.

"So you're gay?" He rocked River, lulling the child.

"I am." Charlie smiled. "I'm out, too. Makes being the head of the country more interesting. People expect me to behave a certain way. They think I should be happy all the time and should be easily fooled." He hadn't told anyone any of this, but when he looked at Nathan, he wanted to spill his guts. "I've had so many people try to con me, to tell me I need them in my life and demand money."

"I had no idea." He turned River around and cradled him to his chest as the child fell asleep. "I'm sorry."

"So am I. I didn't get into this role knowing I'd be forced to marry someone. I thought I was just in charge," Charlie said. "But a decree was put in place to ensure either I got married or got out. That's why I was so sad when you saw me and why I didn't tell you who I was at first. It's probably silly, but I wanted to know there was a spark before the glitter of the crown got in the way. It's a bright light I stand in and some people can't see beyond it."

"And Lender?"

"He's the one who gets the crown if I don't marry." He laced his fingers together. "It made me not happy, but relieved that you contacted me. I'm honored that you thought enough of me, despite the argument, to reach out."

"I knew you'd help me."

"Are you still angry with me?" It was too much to ask to think he'd convinced Nathan to come around this fast.

"I am." Nathan continued to rock River in his arms. "I understand why you did what you did, but it rankles me."

"I know. I knew it would be tough." He was still worried Nathan would push him away. "Lender threatened you because he's the next in line for the crown. My sister's little boy is way too young to take over and my stepmother didn't think I could handle being king, so she put this decree in effect to make sure someone held the crown. Lender is rotten, nasty and will stop at nothing to get what he wants—which is why she liked him. Plus, it means my family won't have the crown. Neither she nor Lender wants me to be happy, and after my father divorced her, she wants everyone who upset her to suffer."

"Would he really kill my son?" Nathan murmured.

"Yes." *Without a doubt.* "That's why I'm insisting you stay here. I won't take no for an answer, either. You need protection. That little boy and your nanny need to be safe and I can make that happen."

"And how do you think the people will handle knowing you've got us living here?" Nathan slowly stopped rocking the baby. "Won't someone question my being here?"

"Probably." He had to think fast. Lender would be the first to question Nathan moving in. "We're getting married," he blurted. It wasn't the best answer, but it'd work.

"What?" Nathan paled. "*Married?*"

"Yes. You and I are engaged as of now and that's why you're moving in — to get used to the castle and life here." He nodded. "Because of the time constraints, we know it's the right decision and I want you here getting settled in." The more he spoke, the more he believed his own lie.

"Charlie, we can't."

"You'd rather risk Lender trying something? Here, I can protect you. I can't be sure he won't get to you at the apartment." He'd try, though.

"I don't have much of a choice, do I?"

He paused. *Shit.* He didn't want to force Nathan, despite thinking this would work. "You have all the choices. Nathan, you don't have to marry me. It was just a story, but I refuse to make you be my husband if it isn't what you'd like. It's a good cover if you're in on the story, but if you're not, then it won't work."

"I can't."

Fuck. "Will you stay here? Just stay until the end of the year and I'll figure something out." He couldn't let Nathan go. "At least give us some time to figure out if we're good together. We might be."

Nathan didn't speak right away. He seemed to be considering what Charlie had said and finally met Charlie's gaze. "You can tell everyone we're getting married, but I want time."

"I can only give you through December thirty-first. I wish I could give you more." He wanted to be with Nathan, and if he had the power to change the situation, he would.

"Here's what I want," Nathan said. "Trust me."

Here we go. Charlie braced himself for Nathan's answer.

"I'm scared Lender will take what's important to me. I'm scared he'll kill River, Mrs. Major or me. It's not right and I doubt he'll stop just because we've announced our engagement. I think he'll try harder to split us up, and I don't want his country ruled by someone who behaves that way. It's not right, either. You seem fair and just," Nathan said. "So we try to make this work. We tell everyone we're engaged and getting married on the thirty-first, but I want the caveat that this might not work now that we've been thrown together and we'll need time to figure things out. I don't want you to hate me if this doesn't work. I like you as a friend and I don't want anything from you other than for us to be honest."

"I agree." He could handle Nathan's demands.

"Do you because you're under duress?" Nathan rubbed River's back. "If you have doubts, then speak up."

"I will, but I don't have any doubts." He palmed Nathan's thigh and could've sworn he felt a jolt—like static electricity through his system. He hadn't kissed this man, hadn't held him, but felt a connection. He had a partner in Nathan—if he could get this to work and last.

"Then let's try." Nathan smiled. The warmth of the gesture reached his eyes. "But know this—River and I are a package deal. Love me, love my son."

"I never thought otherwise." He'd already started falling for them both. He embraced the chance to get to know them and forge a bond.

"Then I'll stay. Mrs. Major does too, right?"

"Absolutely." If things went well, he'd keep Mrs. Major on as the royal nanny. "Did you know her husband was in my father's guard? He died for my father."

"She didn't tell me that." Nathan sagged in his seat. "Wow."

"Yep. I have a soft spot for her because I know what she went through."

Nathan yawned. "Where is the suite? I'm getting tired and he's getting heavy." He stood. "You'd be surprised how fast he gets heavy."

"I've held my nephew." Charlie stood. "The suite is this way." He led Nathan through the castle to the guest suite. Spencer was waiting in the corridor and Charlie spoke to him. "How are things?"

"We got most of the belongings out before Lender showed up," Spencer said. "He did make his presence known and threatened us. He tried to destroy some of the baby items—the crib for one—and we had to replace it, but that was it. Everything else survived and is in the suite. We swept for tracking devices on the furniture and found two in the apartment, in the corner of the ceiling in the living room." He opened the door for Charlie and Nathan. "If you need anything, please let me know."

"I will." Nathan ventured into the suite. "Wow."

Charlie hesitated in the corridor with Spencer. "Okay, what happened?"

"We moved everything out, but Lender was there at the end. He looked angry and demanded to know what we were doing. I said we were helping with a royal move, and that pissed him off even more. When I refused to give details, he destroyed the crib. If you don't keep them here in the castle, he will do something drastic." Spencer shook his head. "I don't want to see anyone hurt because he's raging."

"Then we don't let Lender get what he wants." Charlie scrubbed both hands over his face. "I don't need this."

"No, but you also can't let him win." Spencer stretched. "Nathan's safe and you need to show him he might be just what you want in a partner."

"He might hate my guts for all this, and I wouldn't blame him." Charlie refused to let Nathan get harmed. "I'm giving him space for now, but if he goes anywhere, he'll have security."

"I assumed you'd do that, so it's already done." Spencer clapped Charlie on the shoulder. "You're trying and that's enough for now. You can't do more than your best."

"Thanks," Charlie said. "I'm going to my office. I have no idea what I'm going to do, but I can't sleep."

"It's understandable. If you need me, shout." Spencer left him in the corridor. "Night. I will have my phone on and am just a call away."

"Thank you." Charlie went in the opposite direction down the hallway. His mind overflowed with thoughts of Nathan. He didn't really know him, yet he had to save him. He cared about Nathan, and his little boy, too. Things were happening fast, but he didn't have much time.

He ventured down to his office and locked himself inside. He'd never get anything done, but at least he wasn't sitting in the silence of his massive suite.

Charlie read through emails and reports from the guards during the incidents with Lender. He hadn't been wrong in his concern over Lender. Anyone who'd threaten a baby was truly dangerous.

He'd gone over the details for the Christmas ball, and the more he read, the more he didn't care. Zara was right—having a gathering to find a husband was ridiculous, but there was the decree. He didn't have much time before the decree would be enacted. He wasn't sure how long he'd stared at the reports when a new email popped into his inbox from the *Royal Rag*.

Damn. He groaned and scanned the text of the message. The *Royal Rag* lived to publish gossip about the family. They never checked their sources and always went for the big scoop—true or not.

We are releasing the story concerning you and Mr. Pratt. Mr. Pratt refused to admit to the relationship, but we have photographic proof. We are running the story regardless, but we wanted to alert you to the press coverage.

"Oh thanks," he mumbled. He closed the lid of his laptop. He didn't like the tabloid paper, but the people of Lysianna loved it.

His phone buzzed with an incoming text. *Jesus.* He hoped the rest of the world wasn't going sideways, too. He checked the identification. *Restricted.* Well, that could be anyone.

I'm sorry.

He frowned. Who was sorry? Lender? Not likely. He wouldn't apologize for anything. Nathan? He needed to send an answer, but if it were Nathan, wouldn't he identify himself?

He sent a return message.

For what?

The phone buzzed almost immediately with another text.

Getting angry. This is all a mess.

It is, he sent back. He wasn't sure who was conversing with him. He wished he'd jotted down Nathan's number. He sent another text. He had to keep the conversation open-ended until he knew who sent him the messages.

Don't worry about it.

Another message showed up.

I feel better.

The answer didn't seem like Nathan. He'd been pretty freaked out. A simple text conversation wasn't going to fix it or reassure him that fast.

He didn't want to bother Spencer and refused to annoy Nathan again. He'd have to let the text conversation ride for now. But...the tech team was available and working around the clock.

Charlie placed a call on the private royal line. "I need confirmation of a number. Will you send a tech up to handle it?"

Within ten minutes, one of the techs had Charlie's cell phone and whisked it off to do their digital wizardry.

Not having his phone felt odd, but not completely foreign. He hadn't had a cell phone when he was a kid. The security was different, too. But he was in the castle and safe for now.

Charlie left the office and wandered through the castle to the grand hall. Soon, the ballroom would be full of people, music and action. So many people would be staring at him. A few would try to gain his favor. Maybe it was a ridiculous pipe dream to think he'd find a husband at the ball, or even before the end of the year. There might not even be someone of marriage or partner material there. People would be all over. Women in glittery dresses, men in fine tuxedoes, huge sprays of flowers and gigantic spreads of food. The music, the excitement and dancing...he'd have a fine time, even if he didn't have a chance at finding a husband.

Unless he had a chance with Nathan.

He paused. Lender had pushed him and Nathan together, and that didn't mean he couldn't try to romance Nathan while he was there.

"Oh." The voice echoed. "Wow."

Charlie whipped around. Nathan stood at the other end of the room. "Hi," Charlie called. "Nathan?"

Nathan seemed not to see or hear him, so Charlie crossed the expanse. The move felt rather symbolic — the cavern between them was almost as big as the hall.

"Hi." Charlie shoved his hands into his pockets to hide the trembling. The soft lighting added to Nathan's sex appeal. He could see them dancing together in this room. He didn't need anyone else — just them.

Nathan met Charlie's gaze. "This is crazy."

"It's the ballroom. We like it." Well, he had little choice but to like it. "This room is five hundred years old."

"I believe it." Nathan stood beside him. "All original plaster work, six fireplaces…is the wood carving along the ceiling original, too?"

"Last I checked, it is. My father hated having anything in here because it's a pain in the ass to heat." Charlie glanced at Nathan. The poor man was a bit disheveled, but still sexy, and reminded him of a professor. "You seem to know a lot about the room. I take it you've studied art?"

"As my minor." Nathan half-smiled. "I majored in restoration, but went the extra semesters to get my degree in education and studied art history all the while. I love the old castles and buildings. There are some nice old structures in Cleveland, but when the millionaires on Euclid Avenue died, many of them razed their homes to keep them from decay or falling into the wrong hands. A couple remain, but they're nothing like this."

"You're from Cleveland?" He'd been there once for his sister, but hadn't had the chance to explore the area much.

"I grew up in Bay Village and went to college in Cleveland." Nathan inched away from him. "When I was in college, I realized I was gay. I told my parents and they ignored it. When I brought home my first steady boyfriend, they threw us out. Deeply religious people, they are. I was told to never come back. They don't know about River, that I graduated, that I'm alive..."

"I'm sorry." He hesitated, then grasped Nathan's hand. "Is that why you came here?"

"I wanted a fresh start, yeah." Nathan didn't pull away. "That and River's surrogate is from here. She insisted we have no contact until he's seven years old so he can decide if he wants to meet her."

"Ah." He couldn't imagine not wanting to see his child, but he'd never been a surrogate. "Is she still living here?"

"She moved to Rome with her new husband." Nathan squeezed Charlie's hand. "I see her point. The kid should be able to make some decisions." He said nothing for a bit, then sighed. "Thanks."

"For what?"

"Helping us. I'd just argued with you and thrown you out of my house, but you still came to my rescue. That's huge," Nathan said. "Most guys wouldn't."

"You needed help." He tugged lightly on Nathan's hand, inching him closer. "You texted me to say thanks."

"I did?" Nathan frowned. "Spencer took my phone when we were in the suite. He said he needed to clean it or something."

"To check for bugs or anything else strange in it, I'd bet," Charlie said. "Then you didn't text me?"

"Not yet. I wasn't sure how to contact you." Nathan rubbed the back of Charlie's hand. "Did I say something intelligent?"

"Just that you were sorry." Now he knew the truth — it wasn't Nathan. "I'd rather you told me in person than a text. It's more personal."

"I'd rather say it that way, too," Nathan replied. "So you're the king."

"I am." He held both of Nathan's hands. "Can we start over? We're both in the castle and it might do us some good to be friends." Or more.

"Do you really have to get married? The Lender thing isn't a joke?" Nathan swayed a bit.

"It's not a farce. My stepmother didn't like the idea of me being king or my sister becoming the queen, so she put in roadblocks. She hated that she'd lost control of my father, too." He still remembered the shouting matches. "He thought she loved him, but she loved power."

"Ah. She was one of those." Nathan continued to sway. "I feel like I should be dancing here. I guess it's the lighting."

"Or the room." Charlie swayed with him. "My sister and I used to come in here and shout because of the acoustics."

"I bet." Nathan raised his hands, lacing his fingers with Charlie's and touching palm to palm. "I don't usually let people meet River."

"I didn't think you did." He moved closer to Nathan until he felt Nathan's breath on his skin. He noticed the variations of brown in his dark eyes.

"I try to be cautious. He's little and not everyone has good intentions," Nathan said. "It's crazy. I saw you and I wanted to try, even though I knew better. After Mack, I thought I'd never find someone."

"Then you found me?" He eased his arms around Nathan. "No one ever approached me to talk. No one, except Spencer, cared enough to check on me."

"You sister probably keeps tabs."

"She does." He liked holding Nathan. They fit together well. "Speaking of checking, why were you out strolling? Don't you like it here?"

"Am I a prisoner?"

"No. I can't guarantee Lender won't harm you outside of the castle, but if you'll trust me for now and stay, then I can ensure your safety."

"I have nowhere to go." Nathan rested his forehead against Charlie's and sighed. "The truth is I'm a mess. I'm overwhelmed, too. We just met and there's so much I don't know, but then Lender threatened me and my son could've been attacked. I'm just done. I don't know what else to do, but I can't rest — if that makes sense. Mrs. Major told me to catnap, but it didn't work. I thought walking might help use up the energy."

"I understand. That's why I went for the run earlier." He studied the play of light in Nathan's eyes and committed the nuances of his face to memory. He wanted to remember the sound of Nathan's voice and the way he smiled.

"I liked seeing you run," Nathan said. His voice turned husky. "It was attractive."

"Yeah?" He rubbed Nathan's back.

"Uh-huh." Nathan groaned. "Being a fake fiancé won't be easy if you keep wearing those pants."

He'd have to remember that. "I do enjoy running." He breathed Nathan in, loving the closeness.

Nathan licked his bottom lip. "I want to kiss you."

"I'd like that too." *More than anything.*

"Charlie?"

"Right here." They were so close. He should just kiss him.

"Am I permitted to kiss the king?" Nathan asked.

"Very much so." He tipped his head and feathered his mouth over Nathan's. He wanted to bottle this moment—the softness of Nathan's lips, the way the hairs on his chin scraped against Charlie's, the tenderness in the kiss and the sweetness surrounding them. He slid his palm along Nathan's back to the nape of his neck and trailed his fingers through Nathan's short hair. God, he liked touching him.

Nathan broke the connection. "Wow."

"Yeah." Charlie wasn't ready to let go. "I want to do that again."

"Me, too." Nathan hooked his fingers in Charlie's front pockets. "But we're not alone."

"What?" He kept Nathan close, but turned enough to see the interloper. "Spencer?"

"Hi. Yeah. I'm glad to see this." Spencer gestured to them. "But we need to make an announcement. Word has gotten out via the *Royal Rag* that you're with Nathan. It's been reported you're engaged, too. You need to get ahead of this, or at least be in control of the story."

Right now? "Okay. What do you have written up?" Spencer probably hadn't slept and had spent time running through his emails rather than with his boyfriend.

"I've got the general outline, but I need details," Spencer said. "And before you ask, Ren and I aren't getting along. It was either sleep on the sofa or get some work done. I opted to work because the couch is lumpy."

"I'm sorry," Charlie said. He hoped their argument wouldn't last long.

"So, we need to make this announcement official. Ready?" Spencer asked.

Charlie caressed the back of Nathan's head. "Are you ready?" He'd pushed Nathan into going along with his scheme and now he could only pray Nathan would continue with the ruse — at least until he could prove they belonged together.

Chapter Six

Nathan steeled himself for the questions. A few hours ago, he'd thought he'd met a great, but important guy. Then he'd learned the truth about Charlie and the danger surrounding him, too. His son had been at risk, but was now safe because of Charlie. Some people would be overwhelmed.

Most people might have walked away from Charlie, saying the costs were too high.

Charlie's request to pretend to be engaged was different, but not bad. The act gave them all a chance to get to know each other, as Charlie said, and if Nathan had to be forced to marry someone, Charlie wasn't a poor choice. Charlie was good with River and wasn't put off by the fact Nathan had a son. That was huge.

Charlie kept his arm around Nathan. "If you're not ready, we can wait until the morning."

"No." Nathan tucked against Charlie. "What do you want to know?"

"Give me your full name, or at least the one you want in the official announcement." Spencer held the tablet. "Ready when you are."

"Nathan Loudon Pratt. I'm thirty-two years old, a father to River and I've never been married. I'm from Cleveland, Ohio. I've got two degrees and am actively working to become a citizen of Lysianna." He stood tall. Were his answers enough?

"Well…" Spencer tapped furiously and nodded. "Okay, Charlie? We need to add something about how long you've been together."

Charlie exhaled. "How about we keep it as a while? We've known each other for a while and decided that the Christmas season is the best time to take things to the next level."

"To make it permanent," Nathan said. That sounded better.

"Yes." Charlie kissed Nathan's temple. "Exactly."

Spencer continued tapping. "Great. Here." He gave Charlie the device. "You don't have to convince me this is what you want. I can see it. Now go through that and make sure it's correct. We'll publish it in the digital version tonight and I'll get the official proclamation done first thing in the morning for your seal."

"Very good," Charlie said. "I look forward to it." He offered the tablet to Nathan. "Check it over."

Nathan read the document. Considering how quickly Spencer had prepared it, he'd gotten the details all correct. "Looks good."

"Thank you." Spencer fiddled with the tablet. "Then I have your dual approval?"

Charlie held up his hand. "This means you won't have anonymity any longer. At least for a while, you won't be private, so if this is something that's too much for you, then say so. You can back out. I don't blame you if you change your mind."

"I understand." This would help Charlie and keep his family safe. Charlie wasn't a bad guy and the connection was something he wanted to explore. "I'm fine."

Charlie pressed another kiss to Nathan's temple. "Thank you."

"You're welcome." Nathan squeezed Charlie's waist. He liked the way they felt together.

"Publish it," Charlie said. "I'll add the seal in the morning."

Nathan sighed. He'd gone beyond the point of no return, but he had no regrets. Honestly, he was at peace with the situation. Marrying Charlie wasn't awful—not by a long shot.

"You should get some rest," Spencer said. "Things will ramp up tomorrow when the official document goes out. My king, your sister will be angry you didn't tell her first."

"I know." Charlie rubbed Nathan's back. "I'll escort you to your suite."

"Thank you." Nathan appreciated Charlie's tenderness.

"Good evening, Spencer. Now get some rest," Charlie said. "I'll see you bright and early, but not again tonight, yes?"

"I will go to bed once this is posted." Spencer bowed, then turned on his heel and left.

"You should crash, too. Until everything blows over, you'll be in the middle of the craziness. Photographs, interviews, intrusions into your private life and on your time. That's the other reason I insisted on Mrs. Major staying here with you. She'll be a huge help. She'll protect River as much as we will."

"She will." *We.* He liked the sound of that. "Thank you."

"I should be thanking you. You're getting me out of a jam." Charlie walked with him out of the ballroom. "You're getting an entire new family, too. My sister will insist on meeting you. She's protective and she'll want the boys to be playmates."

"I bet so, and that's fine." He was enjoying the stroll with Charlie.

"I need to know something, though. Tell me exactly why you're doing this," Charlie said. "Be honest."

"You don't trust me. You've been burned before, haven't you?"

"Only a dozen times." Charlie stopped in the corridor. "I'm sorry. This is going fast and I'm worried you'll hate me. We don't have to do this. Say so and I'll pull that announcement. I'll take the heat, so don't worry about that."

Nathan smoothed his palms over Charlie's chest. "I honestly have no idea what I'm up against. I've never been a public person. But you are, and we're doing this thing that might not last, but we are. I saw what Lender was capable of when he threatened my family, and I'm about self-preservation, I won't lie. But I'm also about spending time with you and getting to know the guy who is king when he's not being the king. I'm excited to have these moments with you. I expect to be put in a fishbowl, but that's okay because we'll do it together. There is a man in here who is dying to be loved and appreciated. That's the one I want to know. That's the man I want to help because he's genuine. The crown, the publicity…it's not important. You are."

Charlie clasped Nathan's wrists. "This is why I knew we'd be good together. You get what I need."

"It's a gift." Nathan kissed him. "We have three weeks."

"Not even," Charlie said.

"We'll figure this out." Nathan barely knew Charlie, but he trusted him. He'd protect them and Nathan would do the same for Charlie.

"I'll visit you after breakfast," Charlie said and walked Nathan the rest of the way to his suite. "I've got a meeting early, but we'll get a schedule of events created to announce the engagement."

"What about River?" He should've asked before. His life affected River's and he didn't want his son on display yet. "Do you want him present? It'll come out eventually that I'm a dad, but I don't want everyone gawking at him yet."

Charlie slowed his pace. "What do you want to do? This is your son, and if you don't want to subject him to scrutiny, then we won't. I believe it's no one's business to take his photograph until you say so."

He stopped at his suite. "Keep him out of the spotlight right now. We can tell everyone I have a child, but he doesn't need to be in the photos. You can set something up that's official later." If they continued the relationship — which he hoped they did — then that was when he'd introduce the world to River.

"Good enough," Charlie said. "If you have issues or questions, tell me. I want you to be happy. I know it's not a real engagement, but I don't want to hurt you."

"I'll speak up." He wasn't afraid to tell Charlie the truth. He didn't like the way Charlie kept saying this wasn't real. He'd developed feelings for Charlie and didn't want the relationship to end.

"Then good night. I'll ensure you have a phone tomorrow, but you're welcome all over the palace." Charlie curled his fingers under Nathan's chin. "Sleep well."

"Thank you, Charlie." He kissed him. "You're a good man." Anyone would be proud to have Charlie as their husband and he wanted more than anything for this engagement to be real. The more time he spent with Charlie, the more things felt right.

Charlie lingered another second. "Bye."

"Bye." Something stirred in his soul. Was it his heart beating again? Being with Charlie was totally a rush. He stepped into the suite, leaving Charlie in the corridor.

"How'd it go?" Mrs. Major asked. "You were gone quite a while."

"I was."

"You're smiling." She clasped her hands together. "Now do you believe me that he's the king?"

"I do." He settled on the chair. "How's River?"

"Sleeping heavily. The nursery is almost perfect. It's nicer than what you had, which was pretty darn nice, and it's almost exactly what was in the apartment. He took care of us," Mrs. Major said. "Like family."

"I'm sure he did. I'm marrying him, so we'll *be* family."

Her eyes widened as she settled on the chair. "You're serious? Nathan?"

"What?" The sheer importance of what he'd said and done crashed over him. He'd agreed to a fake engagement he wanted to be real.

"You're going to marry the king?" She covered her mouth with her hand. "I'm shocked," she said through her fingers.

"So am I."

"You'll fix his problem," she murmured and dropped her hand.

"Sort of."

"Sort of? I don't understand."

He couldn't tell her the engagement was currently a sham. "It's happening fast."

"What about River?"

"He's not to be photographed until Charlie and I approve of it."

"Good. He shouldn't be in the middle," she said.

"No." At least not until Nathan convinced Charlie they belonged together.

"Then okay." She stood. "I'm going to bed."

"Mrs. Major? Will you stay on as River's nanny if I do marry Charlie?" Nathan remained seated. "I'd love for you to stay. I already mentioned it to Charlie and he loves the idea."

"Me? In service of the king?" Tears streamed down her cheeks. "You asked him to keep me on?"

"If you want to stay on." He hoped so.

"I would be honored." She threw herself into his arms and hugged him. "Thank you, Nathan."

"Welcome." He stood and hugged her back. "Get some sleep. We're going to have a big day tomorrow." *And for the next three weeks.*

"We will." She let go and practically skipped out of the room.

He switched off the lights and locked the suite door before heading to his bedroom. The large doors between his room and the nursery were open. He could see River and hear if he had problems. *Good.* Nathan brushed his teeth and changed. He couldn't wrap his mind around the fact that he was in a castle and now seeing a king. He'd never thought his life would go in this direction. He wasn't important. He'd simply seen Charlie at a rough moment and tried to be kind.

Now, he lived in the royal visitors' suite. He donned a pair of sleep shorts, then checked on River before falling into bed. Bone-deep weariness along with excitement shot through his veins.

He'd made the boldest choice. He was safe and his family was, too. He'd begun to fall for Charlie, as well.

He stared at the ceiling. Mrs. Major had said Charlie had been used and he'd mentioned it, too. *Why would someone want to do that?* Charlie was a nice guy, sweet, caring and funny. How could someone use him? Whoever it was, the person must've been a rotten soul.

Why did he think he was already starting to fall in love with Charlie? What was it about him that had made the seed start to grow?

Seeing Charlie in that running suit had certainly helped. It was like a glimpse at a package to unwrap and the anticipation would kill him, but he didn't care. Then there was the kiss. Touching Charlie blew his mind. It was so exciting and new. He'd never get enough. But the most important thing was the way Charlie had jumped in to help him. Nathan hadn't asked for a suite in the palace. He'd wanted safety and Charlie had granted it without question.

Only a man of integrity would do such a thing.

Yes, he felt indebted to Charlie, but more than that, he wanted to show Charlie that real love existed, that not everyone was out to get something from him.

But he'd expected something — protection.

Shit.

He'd have to prove the fake engagement could be real. Charlie believed he couldn't be loved for himself, but he was wrong. He deserved whatever he wanted and Nathan wouldn't stop until he showed Charlie he was the best thing to happen to him.

* * * *

When Nathan woke, he gave himself a few seconds for the fog of sleep to clear, then sat up. If he wanted to properly romance Charlie, he'd have to start today.

He dressed in sweatpants and a T-shirt, then ventured out to the living room. He hadn't heard River all night.

Mrs. Major was at the table with River sitting in a highchair. "They thought of everything," she said. "We've even got cereal for River. The king is doing his best to charm us."

"He is." He ruffled River's short hair. "He slept well. So well I never heard him."

"You were pretty tired when you came back." She fed the child more of the cereal. "He woke around seven-thirty and was playing with his squeaky bunny, but you were out."

He settled on the other chair at the table. "I had a wonderful evening." He'd never felt this wistful about being out, especially when it wasn't even a date.

"Wandering the castle? It's a wonder you didn't get arrested." She wiped River's chin. "Did you get caught?"

"In a matter of speaking, I did. I spent part of the evening with Charlie." He sighed. His heart lightened and his spirits lifted. "It's hard to understand, but we found each other and it felt right. He's sweet and caring...until I mentioned that him being the king didn't strike me as obvious."

"I know." She cleaned off the rest of River's face. "He's been good for the country, but he's very low-key."

"I really like him."

"You're going to marry him, so it helps if you do." She stood and wiped down the high chair as River played with the teething ring. "Right?"

"Yes." He had to admit the truth, though. "The engagement isn't really...real."

"What?" She froze. "You're kidding."

"When Lender threatened us, Charlie and I decided we needed a story to get Lender to back off. Saying we're engaged made sense," he said. "There's a story that's going to be in the *Royal Rag* — I think that's what it's called — outing us, so we just went with it."

"The *Royal Rag* is junk." She left the table and rinsed out the cloth. "I don't trust it."

"Charlie and I discussed the decision and it was mutual." He freed River from the high chair and plopped him on his lap. "I know Charlie's in a bind, and a farce engagement won't help much, but I do like him. Not because he's the king, but because he's Charlie. I don't want the engagement to be fake."

She nodded. "So you're hoping the lie becomes the truth."

"Yes. Is that bad?"

"No." She smiled and draped the rag on the rack. "It's a good thing you've been thrown together."

He hugged River. "I started liking him before I knew what was happening."

"That's better." She folded her arms.

"What is? The truth?"

"It is, because it's high time you admitted it. I could see it in your eyes." She leaned against the counter.

"You deserve to be happy and Mack was terrible for you. You needed to move on."

"I am." Mack wasn't even a fleeting thought in his mind.

She handed River the teething ring, but before she could speak, someone knocked on the suite door. She answered and opened the door. "Hello?"

Spencer strode into the room. "I have your phones. They're both clean and have been enhanced with extra features to keep them secure." He handed over the devices. "I have keys for you as well, and before I forget, the royal team of tailors and seamstresses will be here shortly to measure you. Mrs. Major, you'll be selecting fabric and a style for your ball gown. Nathan, you'll be measured for three complete suits and a tuxedo."

"Suits? For what?" He didn't need three.

"The official portraits and events between now and the ball." Spencer fiddled with his tablet. "You'll be doing an official event this afternoon with the king. What do you have for dress clothes?"

"Not much. Do I have to have something fancy?" He held on to River. "I'm a dad, not a fashion plate."

"It wouldn't hurt for you to dress up. You should look assembled and sophisticated, but you don't need a full suit." Spencer frowned. "Let's check your closet."

"There isn't much and I haven't unpacked my bags. What's in the closet is what the staff put there." He followed Spencer into the bedroom. "I'm not good with fashion. I get my plaids mixed with my stripes. I do have a great vest—it went with a suit I had."

"Had?" Spencer yanked the closet doors open. "What happened to it?"

"My ex-boyfriend stole the jacket and pants." He bounced River on his hip. "If I'm permitted to pick for myself, I'd choose the vest, my navy button-down and black slacks. It's classy and goes together, but it's over the top."

"You'll need to wear a tie." Spencer pulled the garments from the closet. "Do you have any neckties?"

"No." He'd never needed one. "Should I get a few?" He wasn't even sure where to shop for such things.

"I'll have some sent up, including one with the family crest. It'll look good for the photo with Charlie. I'll let him know to wear dress casual for this afternoon." Spencer tucked the tablet under his arm. "The tailors should be here in a moment. They know what colors and styles of suit to order, but they need your measurements. Just let them do their job, okay?"

"Sure." He followed Spencer back to the living room. "Thanks? I don't need three suits. I can make one or maybe two work for me. Three seems excessive."

"Three is the minimum you need. One in black, navy and slate gray. You will have plenty of events to dress for and variety is your best friend." Spencer handed Nathan a piece of paper. "This is the official document from the king stating you aren't to work for now. School is complete for the remainder of the month and we've set your student up with a new tutor. You will be permitted to resume your work in the archives in January if you wish."

"Thanks." He brushed River's hair off his face and dried a bit of drool from his chin. The more he watched Spencer, the more he wondered what was wrong with the man. "Lord Spencer?"

"Yes?" Spencer paused. "What's the matter?"

"You don't like me, do you?" He wanted to be accepted by Charlie's team. "I'm not good enough for him, am I?"

Mrs. Major swooped in and took River, then left the room. Spencer cleared his throat. "It's not that I don't like you. I'm leery," Spencer said. "You're not the first person to show up and want to romance the king. You're the first to do it now that he's the king, but that doesn't matter. Prove to us you aren't trying to dick him over and I'll like you a whole lot more. He's not only my king, but my friend. I love him enough to want him to be happy."

He hooked his fingers in his waistband. "Do you love him?" That had to be it. Spencer felt slighted because he wasn't the one marrying the king — his best friend.

"Not romantically," Spencer said. "We grew up together. I've known him longer than almost anyone, but I don't want to sleep with him. Not only are we too similar, but I don't want to be with the king. It's too much pressure and I like being able to walk away at night."

"Ah." That made sense.

"I'm not your rival, but if you make a bad impression, I won't help you," Spencer said. "Got it?"

"Yes, I do." He widened his stance. "Thank you."

"Welcome." Spencer sighed. "The tailors are here. I'll be outside if you need me." He paused. "One more thing. You are to meet with Charlie at two-thirty in his office. Be dressed and ready for your first official presentation. You will be photographed, so comb your hair. You need to look like you belong with royalty."

"No pressure."

"Not at all." Spencer smiled. "Charlie likes you because you're yourself. Be you and let that shine. The people will accept you more if you're genuine."

"I can do that." He didn't have much choice. He liked Charlie and wanted to make him happy. "I'll be there."

"Good." Spencer opened the door. A group of people, complete with tape measures, chalk and each holding a tablet, ventured into the suite. Spencer pointed to his watch. "Be ready at two-thirty."

"I will." Nathan faced the army of tailors and braced himself for whatever came next. He might as well get used to the swarming people and action. He had the feeling Charlie dealt with it all the time.

Right now, he wanted to make Charlie proud.

Chapter Seven

Charlie finished his meeting and rushed through lunch. He hated not being able to see Nathan, especially since he'd promised he'd visit.

Spencer rushed into the office. "A moment?"

"Sure." He sank onto his chair again. "What fell apart?" So far, nothing had gone right today. The flight carrying his sister and family had been delayed, his father was still on the diplomatic visit and not expected to be at the announcement, plus Lender hadn't been spotted in twenty-four hours. Charlie wanted him under constant surveillance.

"Nathan's been sorted out with three new suits and fitted for his tuxedo. He's not picky — which is good — and I helped him select an outfit for the announcement. He should be here in half an hour, like I put on the schedule." Spencer pointed to his tablet. "It's last-minute, but the press is clamoring to be there."

"You gave me almost no time to get ready. I look like shit." Sometimes he appreciated Spencer's thorough approach, but right now he wanted to wring his neck.

"You look fine." Spencer stood behind him. "Comb." When Charlie gave him the tool, Spencer set to work combing Charlie's hair. "I chatted with him, too."

"Oh?" Charlie tensed. "And?" Spencer could be too blunt for his own good.

"Actually, it was a pleasant chat. I didn't threaten him," Spencer said. "That's better. Your hair looks fine. Stand, so I can fix your clothes."

Charlie complied. "What did you tell him?"

"Not to screw up." Spencer adjusted Charlie's shirt, then collar. He picked up Charlie's jacket. "Wear this and let me look at you."

Charlie donned the garment. "What did you discuss?"

"You." Spencer stepped back and folded his arms. "He didn't beg for a bunch of new clothes and really does live simply. He takes care of his son and wasn't interested in money. He said he didn't see why he needed three suits." He squinted. "Good. I got him a tie, but I'll get him a few more sent over. You should look great together. Have you chosen a ring?"

If he hadn't known Spencer for most of his life, he'd be jarred by Spencer's style of conversation. Only Spencer could switch topics so fast and expect him to keep up. He pointed to Spencer. "I did pick a ring. In fact, I want him to have the one my grandfather wore."

"The ruby? Isn't it big?" Spencer continued to frown. "I guess it is an engagement ring."

"It's low-set and not overly ostentatious." He opened the jewelry box. "See?"

Spencer's expression changed and softened. "It's good." He slowly smiled. "Do you like him? I mean, really like him?"

"I think so." Charlie closed the box and tucked it into his pocket. "It's new and fast, but I feel a connection. I didn't want to leave him last night and it's killing me to not see him now. When I kissed him, it was magic."

"I saw."

"But?" Spencer always had an argument.

"No buts. I don't want you to get hurt, though." Spencer rested his hands on his hips. "I have a good feeling about this."

Would Spencer still have such a positive vibe once he learned that Charlie had originally decided the engagement would be fake? "So do I." Charlie checked his watch. There were still twenty minutes until Nathan would be there. "This isn't real, though. Why am I nervous?"

Spencer glared at him. "What do you mean—this isn't real? What are you talking about?"

"Nathan and I aren't really engaged. It's sort of a play to get Lender to fuck off." Charlie shrugged. "We barely know each other." If he kept telling himself the lie, maybe he wouldn't believe it.

"You ass."

Charlie snorted. "Excuse me?"

"You ass," Spencer said. "That man is starting to fall for you. He didn't beg for clothes, isn't screaming for extra stuff and wants the best for you. That's not something you come by often."

He stared at Spencer. On one hand, he didn't like being called such names. He wasn't an ass. On the other hand, Spencer spoke the truth. He'd found a gem in Nathan.

"Well?" Spencer's jaw tensed. "You're serious about this being fake?"

"What should I do?" He'd love Spencer's thoughts on this one.

"Romance him," Spencer snapped. "Charlie, you have a rare treasure and a deadline. You can't afford to do something fake. Plus, you wouldn't have picked out that ring if you thought this was a farce."

True. "Spencer, I do like him and things are falling into place. I wouldn't wish Lender's wrath on anyone, but it did get Nathan and me together faster."

"Good. But you're afraid." Spencer folded his arms again. "Right?"

"Yeah. If I give my heart, what do I do when he breaks it?" He hated admitting that out loud.

"What if he doesn't?"

"What if it falls apart?" Charlie countered.

"What if that's not the future for you?" Spencer asked. "Charlie, you've been burned, but not everyone is out to steal from you. I don't want anything from you and I'm still here. He could be the same way."

"True." He squared his shoulders. "It's December sixth, right?"

"The last time I checked, it was."

He counted on his fingers. "I have just under three weeks until the ball. Do you think I'll know if he's the one by then?"

"You'll only know if you try." Spencer fixed Charlie's collar again. "Try."

"I will." He looked at himself in the mirror. "Not too bad. I could almost pass for kingly."

"You do." Spencer left him at the mirror. "I don't know about kingly, but you don't look half bad. You're right, that combination does work."

Charlie noticed Nathan's reflection in the mirror. He whipped around to gaze at him properly. "Hi."

"Hi." Nathan tugged at the hem of his vest. "Am I okay? Really?"

"More than okay." He forgot about Spencer being in the room and bridged the gap to Nathan. "I'm impressed and I like it."

"You're not too bad yourself." Nathan smiled and reached for Charlie. "What do we do now?"

"This." Charlie let go and dropped to one knee. "Nathan Pratt, I'd be honored if you'd marry me. Will you?" He withdrew the box and opened the lid.

Nathan's lips parted as he smiled. "Charlie?"

"We can't get married unless I ask you," Charlie said. "Thought I'd do this right."

"I will marry you," Nathan said. "I'd be honored."

He slipped the ring onto Nathan's finger and marveled at the perfect fit. The coincidence wasn't lost on him. He stood at his full height. "I hoped you'd agree."

"Why not? I like you, Charlie." He held Charlie's hands. "Fake or not, I want to do this."

Charlie wanted to tell Nathan this wasn't a farce any longer, but the words wouldn't come.

Spencer applauded. "This is so beautiful, I could cry. I won't, but I could. Now, it's time to get the photos done and tell the public yourselves that this is happening. I'll be right back." He left them alone in Charlie's office.

"You look fantastic," Charlie said. Nathan reminded Charlie of a professor or young businessman out on his first date. He longed to kiss him and feel the planes of his body. His mouth watered.

Nathan crossed the expanse to him and slid his hands under Charlie's jacket. "I crave you." He pinned Charlie between his body and the desk. The power move both shocked and excited Charlie. He embraced Nathan. The magnetic pull between him and Nathan was too strong to ignore.

Nathan kissed him. The sheer speed of his action overwhelmed Charlie, but after a second, he kissed Nathan back with ferocity. He caressed the expanse of Nathan's back, then around to his chest. The tautness of his body was evident. Nathan seemed fragile, but was indeed quite tough.

He loved touching Nathan. The man intoxicated him. He could see himself and Nathan being a permanent couple, and he wanted that fantasy to become reality.

Nathan caressed his way down Charlie's body to his cock. Without removing a bit of clothing, he fondled and excited Charlie.

Blood rushed to his erection. All he wanted was to take this man to the closest bedroom and fuck until they couldn't breathe. Hell, he'd like to take Nathan across his desk, too.

He ground on Nathan, needing the pressure and release. Nathan brought out something primal within him.

"Okay, let's head —" Spencer broke off and growled. "You'll muss yourselves."

Nathan remained close, but broke the kiss. "We've been interrupted."

"Sure have." Charlie panted. He'd forgotten about the photo op. Nothing seemed to matter except being with Nathan. He'd never experienced anything this all-consuming before.

"Get yourselves under control." Spencer plunked the tablet on the desk. "You need to fix your hair and clothes...and put those away."

Charlie's cheeks and the tips of his ears burned. He knew what Spencer meant and willed his erection to wilt a bit. "Sorry."

Nathan backed up and adjusted his trousers. He raked his fingers through his hair. "Sorry, Lord Spencer." The bulge was still evident behind his zipper.

Spencer fixed Nathan's hair, then adjusted his shirt. "You need to have decorum. Christ. You're about the be seen by the whole country."

"I know." Charlie rearranged his shirt and jacket. He stole glances at Nathan. He'd never been this caught up before and liked it.

Nathan blushed. "Sorry."

"You should be." Spencer brushed imaginary dust off Charlie's shoulders. "You're both to represent the country. You can't act like horny toads."

"I'm sorry." Nathan fiddled with his vest. "I'm ready."

As Nathan moved, Charlie caught sight of his grandfather's ring on Nathan's finger. A shiver ran the length of his spine. The ring looked perfect, as if it had been made for Nathan.

Spencer applauded. "Ready? It's time, and I'm not leaving you alone to muss each other again."

Charlie offered his arm to Nathan. "Ready?"

Nathan smiled laced his fingers with Charlie's. "Ready." He stuck close to Charlie's side. "I'm scared, but yeah, I'm ready."

"I'm here." Charlie led the way through the corridor to the solarium, then out to the patio and courtyard. He'd forgotten how much the media scrambled to see the royal family, especially during important events. Nathan trembled slightly and Charlie draped his arm around his waist.

Spencer stood in front of them. "Introducing King Charles of Lysianna and his fiancé, Mr. Nathan Pratt of Cleveland, Ohio." He stepped aside and flashes popped around Charlie and Nathan.

Charlie stiffened his spine. He remembered the crush when his sister had presented Luke to the people. He had to be strong for Nathan now. "We will answer your questions, but be polite."

A male reporter held up his phone. "Are you happy you're going to retain the crown?"

Charlie dipped his head once. "Of course."

"Are you in love?" a female reporter asked. "It's so sudden."

"We are." He squeezed Nathan's shoulder. "When we met, I knew he was the one." The words felt even more true at this moment.

"You've given him your grandfather's ring," another male reporter said. "How do you know he'll live up to that reputation?"

Nathan bristled and Charlie intervened. *What kind of question is that?* "My grandfather would've loved him, so I think it'll be fine," Charlie said.

"Mr. Pratt, you're a commoner and foreigner. What makes you worthy of the king?" another reporter asked.

Nathan hesitated before answering. "I don't know that anyone is truly worthy of the king, but I'll do my best to make him happy."

A male reporter wearing a ballcap waved. "My king, how do you know you'll be able to carry on with your royal duties while planning a wedding? Won't your attention be diverted? How do we know you also won't go over budget and waste taxpayer money on these events?"

Jesus. Charlie continued to hold on to Nathan for support. He had to be diplomatic, despite wanting to chew the reporter out. "We will be combining the wedding and Christmas ball into one event, thus saving money and helping focus my attention on the country."

He listened to a few more questions as Spencer took over the press conference. God, the reporters were being nosy today. He expected the rush of photos, but not so many probing queries.

"One more question, my king," a woman said. "You believed you were in love before and planned to marry. How is this relationship different and how do you know it will last? Won't we be better off allowing you to take your time in finding a partner while Count Lender rules? This man seems rather unsuitable."

He should've guessed someone would ask such things and be negative. "I trust my judgment and know my heart. I'm doing what I believe is best for the country. Thank you."

He escorted Nathan into the solarium, and when Spencer shut the door, Charlie kept the smile on his face. "Don't let your cheery expression fade," Charlie said. "They're still watching us."

"Right." Nathan held Charlie's hand. The smile seemed genuine, but the tone of his voice proved his fear. "They ask rough questions, don't they? Are they always so invasive?"

"Only when Lender plants people in the crowd." Charlie embraced him. "I wouldn't worry."

Spencer gestured to the doorway. "We've set it up for the official portrait to be taken in the royal sitting room. It's all ready for you, so we can go up there now. Once we're finished, the princess and prince have arrived with the future king and would like to meet your fiancé. Would you like me to retrieve Mrs. Major and the child for this visit?"

Charlie met Nathan's gaze. "Your call."

"Sure." Nathan exhaled. "It's strange not to have River here, but with him and Mrs. Major, my stand-in parent figure, it'll be fine."

"Then she should be here." Charlie palmed Nathan's ass. "It's going to be impossible to keep my hands off you."

"Likewise." Nathan tucked against Charlie's side. "I have to confess, I hate getting my photo taken."

"The guy photographing us is the prince—my sister's husband—so we're in good hands." Charlie lagged a few steps behind Spencer. He knew the way to the royal sitting room and didn't need an escort.

"What's wrong?" Nathan murmured. He stopped walking. "Charlie?"

He needed to add more romance to this moment and not so much formality. "Have dinner with me tonight? You and River and Mrs. Major." He actually wanted Nathan to himself, but they had to work up to it.

"Like dinner or a date?" Nathan held on to Charlie's hands. "I'd love to share dinner with you every night."

"Regular family dinner tonight and a date tomorrow? We need to spend time together and I know that doing so means getting to know River as well." He wanted them to be a family.

"I'd like that." Nathan's eyes shimmered. "A lot."

"But that doesn't mean I don't want to continue what we started in my office." He kissed Nathan. "That's the hottest thing to ever happen in that room."

"It's hard to keep my hands to myself when it comes to you." Nathan threaded his arms around Charlie's waist. "Let's get this photo done so we can have some private time we don't have to steal."

"Good point." He kept Nathan close and ventured up to the royal sitting room. *Time for the family chaos to begin.*

Charlie stopped just outside the room. "Couple things. My sister will hug you. She loves to hug people. Luke is a great guy and reserved. Zara, my sister, will want to hold River, too. Because it's me and you, she might be pushier than she would with others. It's okay, but if you feel overwhelmed or want air, just tell me."

"She loves you and I can handle that. I'm not used to clingy family, but it'll be fine." Nathan held on to Charlie's arm. "Let's do this."

Charlie opened the door. Spencer was chatting with Luke and Zara held Alistair. Mrs. Major stood at the edge of the space with River.

"There he is," Zara said. She rushed over to Charlie. "I should be mad at you for holding out, but I'm too happy." She sighed as Nathan abandoned them for River.

"He's protective of his son." Charlie hugged her. "I'm glad you made it."

"I wouldn't have missed this for anything." She offered Alistair to him. "So, a single dad. I like it. How did this all happen? I want details."

"It sort of just fell into place. I looked up and he was there." Charlie toyed with his nephew's small hand. "It wasn't what I expected, but I'm not arguing."

"He's the one you told me about, isn't he?"

"Yes."

"Good. I knew he'd be special because you mentioned him. You never talk about your boyfriends." She wiped crumbs from Alistair's shirt. "Do you love him?"

"My nephew or my fiancé?" Charlie asked, knowing full well what she meant.

"Both would be nice." She crooked her eyebrow. "Charlie?"

"I love your son as if he were my own. With Nathan, things happened at warp speed, but I do." He hadn't seen anything to make him question his feelings. Sure, the situation was ridiculous and the timeframe had been enhanced, but he cared so much for Nathan.

"That's what I wanted to hear." She took the child from Charlie. "Get this photo done. We should be celebrating, not sitting all stiff for a picture."

"We should." He wanted to get this done and himself married to Nathan so he could focus on their future as well as running the country.

Chapter Eight

Nathan sank onto the sofa and held River. He still detested getting his photo taken, but he'd never posed for so damn many shots before, either. He liked Zara and Luke, but they'd enjoyed the photo session more than he'd ever like it. Plus, he'd never seen so much food in his life. Once Zara had told the staff to bring up dinner, the trays had seemed not to stop. *Who needs so much to eat?*

Charlie sat beside him. "Overwhelmed yet?"

"I passed that about an hour ago." He rested his head on Charlie's shoulder. He could take a nap while River snoozed on his chest. "They're all so full of energy."

"Zara's excited. We were pretty much shut off from the world as kids and she loves family." Charlie palmed Nathan's thigh. "I'm enjoying everyone being here, though. I miss the family noise in the castle. It's been too quiet."

"You thrive on chaos." He breathed in the scent of Charlie and allowed the woodsy aroma to calm him.

"I'm not sure I like the upheaval, but it goes with you, so I'll live."

"The attention can be overwhelming — and speaking of attention, the official photos of us have gone wide. Everyone knows who you are and that this is happening," Charlie said. "You're trending."

"Oh God." Good thing he'd kept his social media clean. He'd intentionally not posted pictures of River and didn't mention him much. He'd rather just post things about animals and being happy with life. No one needed to read his bitching in post form.

"Don't worry about it. You're insulated here. People can look you up, but they can't get close," Charlie said. "I promise things will be contained."

He'd known getting engaged to Charlie would bring unique problems, but he'd agreed to take on this role. He couldn't complain about the mess if he were partially responsible.

Mrs. Major ventured up to them. "Mind if I put him to bed?"

"I'll go with." Nathan managed to stand and kept River in his arms. "Are there protocols for us now, Charlie? Like, should I be bowing to you? Do we have to sleep in separate quarters? Am I permitted to visit you?" He had no idea what to do.

"There are protocols, but I'm the king and I can change those to suit my mood, so no, you don't have to bow to me right now. At official functions, you'll be expected to. We can sleep in the same quarters, but I wasn't sure if you were ready to take that step, and you can visit me whenever you like." Charlie rubbed Nathan's back. "I'll come with you to your suite so you can be with your son and we can continue to talk."

"Your sister is here," Nathan said. "She won't mind?"

"Nope." Charlie gestured to Nathan. "I need the time away from the chaos, too. Come on."

With Charlie in the lead, Nathan slipped out of the suite. Mrs. Major walked behind Charlie. Nathan sighed. He appreciated Charlie escorting them or he'd have gotten lost.

Once at the suite, Mrs. Major took River into the nursery.

"Did I say something wrong?" Charlie asked. "I didn't talk."

"She's efficient and she's giving us space," Nathan said. "I might have also asked her about staying on as the royal nanny."

"And she agreed?"

"Sure did." So fast he barely believed it. "I know I overstepped, but I didn't want her to think she was being discharged. I need her, even if I'm not working." He was still a single parent and Charlie wouldn't be much help because of his role.

"You might have overstepped a bit, but I like her and you need the help." Charlie wandered around the room. "I've never been in here. My father kept a tight rein on us when we were kids."

"Do you plan on doing that with your child?" Nathan asked. "I don't want River to grow up with tight boundaries, but I don't want him running wild, either."

"I want my child to attend public school and have a normal life—not that I know what normal is. I don't want him to grow up treating people like garbage because of his position." Charlie continued pacing. "I want my child to have values. I'd like him to grow up better than I did."

"That's what I want for River, too." He stepped into Charlie's path. "What's wrong?"

"What do you mean?" Charlie grasped Nathan's hands. "I'm fine."

"Really? You seem edgy and are pacing the room. Are you having second thoughts?" He sucked in a ragged breath. "Charlie?" Things were going well, but he'd made a misstep or two. If that was what Charlie saw as detrimental, then they needed to talk.

"No second thoughts." Charlie groaned. "I confess, I'm worried."

"About?"

"This is going fast. We told each other it was fake, but the more we're together, I don't know if I want it to be a lie." Charlie rested his forehead against Nathan's and bumped noses with him. "I like you more than I thought."

"Is that bad?" He didn't think so.

"It is if you decide to change your mind."

"Charlie?" He tugged Charlie to the French doors leading to the balcony. "Talk to me. We've got some privacy here and we can see the stars."

Charlie held Nathan's hand and led him to the bedroom. Nathan cracked the door between his room and the nursery, then turned his attention to Charlie, who sat on the edge of the bed.

"I got into this relationship thinking you'd want out right after we marry or you wouldn't go through with it. You'd see the chaos around me and realize it's a lot to handle. It's stifling," Charlie said. "It takes someone with a strong constitution."

"So? Every marriage requires work." He'd put in the time and effort to make this successful.

"People tend to jump ship."

He straddled Charlie's lap and slid his hands beneath Charlie's jacket. "You've met the wrong people," he said. "When I was a kid, my parents didn't show each other much affection. I doubt they liked each other much, to be honest, and I thought that's how people behaved. Then I got to high school and met my friend Henry. He was sweet and caring, but also perceptive. He knew my parents weren't fond of me and I used to spend time at his house. He'd tell me to sleep over and I wouldn't argue because I liked the feeling there. His parents liked each other and him. They showed me what a stable, healthy relationship looks like. Until now, I tried to convince myself the wrong people loved me, but when I look into your eyes, I know this is love. It's fast and new, but it's something deeper than I've ever experienced."

Charlie embraced him. "We know so little about each other."

"Ask me anything." He had nothing to hide.

"When did you lose your virginity?"

The tips of his ears burned. "You're hitting with the hard stuff first, eh? I lost it when I was twenty. I met Walt and thought he was dreamy. It was awkward and over too soon. I don't regret it, but I wish it'd been more memorable. You?"

"I was eighteen and he was twenty-two. I thought he loved me," Charlie said, his voice soft. "He loved attention and I didn't have enough to give him." He paused. "Have you ever had your heart broken?"

"I thought I loved Mack, but I hesitate to give him that much credence, and yes, I had my heart broken. He loved himself and I didn't see it." He caressed Charlie's nipple through the fabric of his shirt. When the sensitive bead tightened, Nathan grinned. "Have you...ever had your heart broken?"

"Not really, but I never gave my heart to anyone," Charlie said. His breathing hitched. "I want you."

"You can have me. We're engaged." He pushed Charlie back on the bed. "I want to be wanted." He stretched out on top of him and kissed him. A spark shot through Nathan. "I want to be craved and adored," he added between kisses.

Charlie groaned. "I can do that." He unbuttoned Nathan's vest, then shirt. Another groan ripped from his throat as he massaged Nathan's bare chest.

Nathan removed his necktie, then shrugged out of the shirt and vest, baring his upper body. He resumed kissing Charlie. The chilly air wrapped around him, but did little to quell his fever. He scooted back and fumbled with Charlie's pants. He needed to touch Charlie everywhere.

"Oh God." Charlie whimpered. "I want you naked."

He popped the button on Charlie's pants, then unfastened his belt and unzipped him. Electricity raced through his veins. The moment he wrapped his fingers around Charlie's shaft, time seemed to slow to a crawl.

A moan rumbled in Charlie's chest. "Yes." He guided Nathan down his body. "Need you."

Nathan settled on his knees at Charlie's feet, then tugged Charlie's pants and boxers down his legs to expose him. He'd imagined what Charlie looked like based on the way the running pants fit his body, but seeing him in his full glory now made Nathan's mouth water.

Charlie propped himself up on his elbows. "Do it." His eyes glittered in the moonlight.

Nathan trailed his fingers along Charlie's leg. He wanted to memorize every second of being with him. He brushed his mouth over Charlie's thigh.

"Tease." Charlie palmed the back of Nathan's head. "I love it."

So did he. Nathan nuzzled the curls at the base of Charlie's shaft. *So soft.* Charlie's erection thrummed against his cheek. The power dynamic thrilled Nathan. He loved to please.

Charlie tugged lightly on Nathan's hair. "More. I need you."

"I will, but you have to be quiet," Nathan said. "Can't be too noisy or you'll wake River up." He wrapped his fingers around Charlie's dick.

"I'll never be able to," Charlie murmured. He writhed, pushing his hips toward Nathan. "Please?"

Nathan brushed the blunt head of Charlie's cock across his lips before plunging his mouth onto Charlie's erection. *So full.* The curls at the base of his shaft tickled his nose.

"Heaven," Charlie whispered. He pulled Nathan's hair, encouraging him. The gentle touch set the pace. Nathan bobbed his head. He pushed to the hilt, then pulled back. At the same time, he fondled Charlie's balls. He wanted Charlie to come apart.

"Nathan." Charlie tensed. "Love it." He whimpered and writhed again beneath Nathan.

Pure pleasure filled Nathan. He enjoyed making his lover happy. He flattened his tongue along the underside of Charlie's shaft. When he swallowed Charlie to the back of his throat, Charlie grunted.

"I'm so close." Charlie tugged harder on Nathan's hair and wriggled his hips. He met Nathan's every move with one of his own.

Nathan bit back a groan. They'd fallen into a steady harmony, one body moving together.

Charlie tensed again and shuddered. He rammed his cock into Nathan's mouth. "Nathan." He held tight to Nathan's hair. "Oh God."

He surged into Nathan as he orgasmed. Instead of pulling back, Nathan held fast and swallowed every drop. He didn't want to miss a thing.

Charlie let go and sagged onto the bed. "Damn."

Nathan licked his lips, then stripped to his boxer shorts. Once nearly naked, he crawled onto the bed with Charlie.

"You've wrung me out," Charlie managed. "I could sleep for days."

"So sleep." Nathan snuggled up to Charlie's side. "Stay with me. You don't have to go."

"I should brief with Spencer to learn my schedule for tomorrow. I know the basics." Charlie scrubbed his hand over his face. "It's a protocol I can't change. It's great for order, but lousy for romance."

"I understand." He'd have to work with that detail for the next time, but he could manage. He rubbed Charlie's leg with the top of his foot. "Do your briefing. We'll have plenty of nights together."

"You didn't come." Charlie rolled onto his side. "I want us to be equal this way. I want you to feel the same highs I did."

"I will." He kissed Charlie. "And you can return the favor tomorrow night."

"Except I'll be in the south county for two nights." Charlie groaned. "I'm expected to meet with the officials there about zoning and commerce. We've had this trip in the works for the last month. I'm sorry."

"Then text me each night and we'll figure something out." He wasn't worried. Charlie was the king and had duties. It wouldn't be different if he had another job that required him to be gone at night. "It'll make the heart grow fonder."

"You're not upset?"

"Not at all. Charlie, this is your job. I'm okay with being in the shadows while you do it." He draped his arm across Charlie's side and squeezed his ass. "Tell me what I need to do to support you and I will. You're not alone, but I'm also not trying to be the king, too. I'm good with riding along the sides."

Charlie nuzzled Nathan's neck. "I'm so thankful I found you. You're the one I've been looking for."

"You're the one I want and the one I didn't know if I'd ever find," Nathan murmured.

Charlie's phone rang and he sat up as he silenced the device. "There's Spencer. He's trying to find me."

"Go." He should be annoyed, but the whole situation was so big and out of control on Charlie's end. "I don't mind."

"You're sure?" Charlie cocked his head. "I wouldn't be leaving if Spencer weren't hunting for me."

"I'm positive." He left the bed. "The sooner you get this done—the meeting—the faster we can move forward and spend more time together." Charlie would probably spend a lot of time away from him and Nathan would have to share him, but he had no choice.

"Okay." Charlie dressed but draped his jacket over his arm. "We will start this again when I'm home."

"I can't wait." He walked with him to the door. "I'll count the hours."

"I hope you do." Charlie placed his hand on the door, but didn't open it. Instead, he stared at Nathan.

"What?"

"Just drinking in the details of your face." Charlie slid his free hand over Nathan's neck to the back of his head and kissed him. "You're more than I ever imagined."

"So are you." He kissed Charlie. Most of him wished Charlie would stay. He knew damn well Charlie would be pulled in multiple directions, but that part of him wanted Charlie to stick around a little longer. They had a private oasis. Why did Spencer have to screw it up?

"Bye," Charlie said, despite not leaving the spot.

"Bye." Nathan held on to Charlie's wrist. He feared the separation would prove this was one gigantic dream. He never wanted this to end.

"I'll be back."

"I know." Nathan hesitated. Here he stood in his boxer shorts while Charlie was dressed. If someone saw them, what would they think?

"I've got to go." Charlie planted a kiss on Nathan's lips.

"You should." If he took much longer, Mrs. Major might check on them.

"I'm leaving." Charlie kissed him.

"Go." Every cell in his body screamed for Charlie to stay.

"I'm gone." Charlie jerked. "I hear Spencer coming."

"Go." Nathan laughed. "Get back soon."

"I will." Charlie released Nathan and slipped into the corridor. "Spencer."

Nathan listened to both men and shut the door to preserve some of his modesty. He leaned against the barrier and his heart raced. He'd accepted the ring and agreed to marry Charlie. Now, he'd experienced him, too.

What a difference a few hours made. He'd fallen in love.

Nathan made his way to his bedroom and tumbled onto the bed. He'd been with the king. His sheets smelled of Charlie's cologne. *What a rush!*

He stared at the ring in the moonlight. He'd never thought he'd get married. Now, he would.

Crazy.

Chapter Nine

Nathan woke in the morning, showered, shaved and joined River and Mrs. Major for breakfast.

"This was delivered," she said and waved to the array of breakfast foods. "I didn't even order anything. It just arrived."

"Charlie probably sent it up. I'll let him know we've got enough." More like too much. He took the spoon and fed River some of the baby cereal. "We can put some in the fridge for tomorrow."

"I'd hope so." She left the table. "The princess requested you meet with her today. When does the king expect to be back? She told me he was going away."

"He's going to the south county for two days." He selected an apple from the basket and polished it on his shirt. "I assume I'll find out when he's leaving if he thinks he'll be gone longer. I'll try to remember to tell him or Spencer not to send up so much food."

"I hope when you see him off, it takes less time than last night." She grinned. "I heard the whole thing."

"We tried to be quiet." *Well, shit.*

"It's nice to see you happy." She cleaned the table. "Spencer left this for you, too. I expect it's the agenda for the next few days."

He turned the tablet around. A list of Charlie's engagements filled the screen. "According to this, I need to hustle to see him off." Why hadn't someone told him before now?

"I'll get River ready and you can take him to see Zara when you return." Mrs. Major wiped the baby's face. "He's thriving here."

"Thanks, and I can tell. He's bubbly and happy." He left the table and dressed in a pullover and jeans. Should he be planning out his attire for these things or dressing for comfort? *Damn.* He could use some help. *Oh well.* He put socks and shoes on, then grabbed his phone. He kissed River on the head. "I'll be back."

"See you in a bit," Mrs. Major called.

He finger-combed his hair as he rushed to Charlie's office. He nearly bumped into Spencer. "Sorry."

Charlie stood in the corridor and smiled. "You made it."

"Just barely." Nathan panted. "I ran almost all the way."

"I can see that." Charlie held Nathan's hand and tugged him to the opposite side of the expansive hallway.

"Did I do something wrong?" Nathan caught his breath. He'd forgotten to brush his teeth before coming to meet Charlie. "I offended someone, didn't I?"

"No." Charlie embraced him. "I'm guessing no one gave you a wake-up call."

"They didn't."

"I'll have a chat with Spencer about that." Charlie hugged him tight. "Soon you'll come with me and things will level off."

"I know." He hooked his fingers into Charlie's jacket pockets. "I'm going to miss you."

"I hope so. I'll miss you, too." He kissed Nathan. "My heart's with you."

"Yeah?" Hearing those words made Nathan's spirits soar, but he had to be cautious. "Still think you'll feel that way when River's up all night teething?"

"Yes." Charlie kissed him again. "It'll be two days and we'll plan the wedding. I can't wait."

"We will." Nathan paused. "It'll be overblown, won't it?" He wasn't a fan of big weddings.

"Probably," Charlie said. "But we can do this our way. We'll plan it when I get back. I'm excited to get it done and move forward with our life together."

Our life together. Charlie kept saying the right things. Nathan held on another moment. "I can't walk you to your car, can I?" He wasn't sure what he could and couldn't do.

"It's just outside." Charlie shrugged. "Spencer will keep you inside."

Tears burned at the corners of Nathan's eyes. He hadn't expected to be so emotional. Charlie would only be gone a few days, not forever. "Go."

Charlie kissed him again. "I will." He placed his hand over Nathan's heart. "I'm a call away and right here if you need me."

"Same for me." He let go as Spencer urged Charlie away. He waved. "Bye."

"Bye, my love." Charlie disappeared into the office.

Letting him go shouldn't be so hard, but Charlie had called him 'my love'. That had to mean something.

"Hi." Zara strolled up to him. "Charlie just left, didn't he?"

"Yeah." He fumbled with his hands. "Do I bow? I've had no instruction on how to address any of you."

"You should bow, but I don't expect it." She threaded her arm around his. "Let's walk."

"Sure." He needed to move. "How are you?"

"Good. It's nice to be back in the palace. I forget how big it is when I'm away." She rubbed his forearm. "I'm assuming you're heading to your room. It's tough when they leave us, isn't it?"

"You can tell I'm upset, can't you?" He sighed. "I miss him already."

"I know. That's why we're walking." She kept rubbing his arm. "You have chosen a terribly hard job."

"I did?"

"My brother isn't an easy man to love. He's busy, important and pulled in a thousand directions." She chuckled. "He's done his own thing, but that almost always lines up with what's required of the crown. He deserves to be king."

"I can tell." He appreciated her sense of calm, but there had to be a reason she'd decided to visit him. "Are you going to lecture me? Spencer already did."

"No." She directed him into a large room. "I thought we'd come in here. It's the throne room and the grandest part of the castle."

"It looks it." He'd never seen so much gold in his life. "Are the jewels all real? Isn't it a bit much?" Every golden candelabra was encrusted with jewels, tapestries covered most of the walls and each bench appeared hand-carved. The marble walls gleamed and the throne shimmered with gold and more inlaid jewels.

"I agree it's too much, but this is exactly what the throne room looked like a hundred-fifty years ago. We've merely restored what was damaged over the years." She shook her head. "Dad wanted to simplify, but the people demanded he keep it this way. No kidding, the grandeur is considered a national treasure. I think it's gaudy."

He shrugged. "If it's what they want, then it is." He'd prefer something pared down, but it wasn't his choice to make.

She sat on one of the carved wooden benches. "These were installed for people waiting to meet with the king. Now they're just here for decoration." She held on to his arm. "You fell for my brother, didn't you?"

He wanted to answer her, but the change in topic stunned him.

"I'm not going to give you hell. I care about my brother and you, too." She smiled. "This isn't an easy life."

He sat with her and fiddled with the ring Charlie had given him. "I do love him. It's silly because it's new and we're going at this the wrong way, but he's magnetic and charming."

"I know." She faced him. "It's hard because he's important, but he's so irresistible. He wants the best for everyone. He's the reason Luke and I got our happy ending. Without him giving Luke the job with the court, he wouldn't have been able to be in the country. Charlie fixed it for us."

"I'm not shocked." He could see Charlie doing everything possible for those he loved.

"I know it's tough now and will get lonely, but don't give up, you know? Give him the best you can and things will be fine." She hugged him. "Plus, you've got me. I will do whatever you need to help this work."

"You don't know me."

"But I know people. When I was in college, I took too many people at face value and got to realize not everyone gives a shit about me. They wanted to use me. It seems strange, but there's a certain look they get in their eyes. Lender has it. Elmore, the bastard that wanted to court me, did too. But you? All I see is love and adoration. Hold on to it."

"I'll try." He wasn't sure of what else he could do.

"It's hard, but you can do it." She patted his leg. "Come on. We'll get the boys together to play. You need to be around more people and relax."

"I do." He'd spent too much time alone or with his son and Mrs. Major. Still, Zara changed subjects too fast for him, but so did Charlie. *Oh well.* He had family again and belonged. He'd take it.

* * * *

Friday night, Nathan's phone rang. He expected to hear from Charlie now that the itinerary had changed and he'd be staying an additional night in the county. He wanted to know what time Charlie might be home in the morning so he could wait for him.

He answered the call. "Hello?"

"Nathan," his mother said. "It *is* you, isn't it?"

He nearly dropped the phone. He hadn't spoken to his mother in eight years, yet she'd called. "Hi."

"Is that all you have to say to your mother?" she asked. "Really?"

He didn't know what she expected for a response. "I'm sorry?"

"You're getting married to a prince and your face is all over the computer, but you can't tell us?" she asked. "Why not?"

He massaged his forehead. "First, he's a king and second, you've ignored me for the better part of a decade. What should I do? You refused to answer the phone, emails and you shut the door in my face the last time I came home."

"That's because you were being difficult," she said. "But this is different."

He sighed and stared out of the window at the empty courtyard. "I don't know how this is different, but what do you want?"

"Tickets to that country would be good, for a start. We could use some money for suitable clothes for the trip to meet your king and accommodations. You'll be rich, so it's time you treated us," she said. "Doesn't the king want to meet your parents?"

"No." He wasn't lying. Charlie hadn't expressed interest in seeing them.

"Why not?" she demanded.

"Mom, you told me I wasn't your son because I'm gay. Did that change because of whom I'm marrying?" he asked. "If that's the reason — he's rich and a king, so he's important and you can overlook your prejudice against me — then don't bother. You cut me deep when you informed me you had no son any longer. You can't be parents when it looks good and not be when it doesn't."

"What do you know about parenting? You can't have children," she snapped.

"I have a son." He'd have told her about River, but she hadn't wanted to speak to him. She also wasn't seeing the deep pain she'd caused by throwing him out of her life.

"Then you're not gay and this king isn't really a king? She's a queen and it's all a misprint? Good," his mother said. "That's better. I knew you weren't gay."

"Mom, I'm still gay and he's very much a king," he said. "I'm not sending tickets, money or anything else, because I don't have any money. The king isn't funding my lifestyle or that of my son." He sank onto the bed as his knees weakened. "I'm sorry." She hadn't asked about the baby, but she'd been happy to think Nathan wasn't gay.

"You'd get married without us there?" she asked.

"Yes." He didn't have to think twice.

"Would you do that to your kid?"

He'd had a feeling she'd ask that. "No, I wouldn't because I'd accept him and be proud that he felt comfortable enough to tell me his truth. I'd show up for him because he's my son, not for the glory of being associated with a king or whatever. I'd give him support because he's my child," he said and his voice cracked.

"When he breaks your heart, you'll change your mind." She hung up, leaving him in stunned silence.

Nathan dropped the phone onto his lap. He couldn't stop the tears. The pain in his heart overwhelmed him. How could someone be so cruel? She wanted stuff from him, to be noticed and have attention lavished on her, but she refused to give him respect.

"Nathan?" Mrs. Major ventured into the bedroom. She was carrying River. "You have a... Are you okay?"

"I'll be all right. What's wrong?" He wiped his cheeks and stood to take River from her. He needed to compose himself. "Hi, big guy."

"You have a visitor." She moved out of the way as Charlie strode into the room. "I'll leave you alone because he's the best to help you with whatever's bothering you. Want me to take River?"

He hugged his son. "No, I'm happy to have him here. Hi, Charlie."

Charlie dropped the box he held and rushed over to Nathan. "You missed me so much you were crying?" He pressed his mouth to River's head. "Nathan?"

"You'd better pick up your box or it'll get crushed." Nathan returned to the bed and plopped River on his lap. "My mother called—that's what's bothering me. I thought it was you, but it wasn't. She requested money and thought I'd give her whatever she wanted because I'm marrying you."

Charlie picked up the box. "She's not getting anything from me, and if she's got an issue with that, she can take it up with me personally. I want our little family to be happy." He sat beside Nathan. "I missed you."

"You're home early." He dried his face and bit back his embarrassment. "I thought you'd be gone another night."

"I should've been. The negotiations were all messed up and no one wanted to talk until I made them listen to each other." Charlie shook his head. "They had grand ideas, but no plans. No one wanted to take the lead and create the plans, either. All they expected was money. I'll give funds if you can show me a plan, but I won't without any idea how you're going to use the cash."

"That makes sense." Nathan sighed to compose himself. "Have you eaten?"

"Not since noon. I wanted to get home to see you and demanded the driver stay on the road instead of taking a break." Charlie opened the box. "This is for you. It's cologne from the south county. They make it there and I thought you might like some."

"Thanks." He placed the box on the bed. "I appreciate it."

"I brought River a bunny, but Mrs. Major insisted we keep it in the nursery." Charlie shrugged. "I'm glad I came home when I did. It looks like you needed me here. I needed you, too."

His world righted with Charlie beside him. Zara was right—he'd fallen in love with Charlie. Once they made love, he'd know for certain just how much he loved the king. He'd found the partner to respect him and the man who accepted him as a package deal.

He couldn't let him go.

Chapter Ten

Charlie finished the last of the popcorn in the bowl. He hadn't shared popcorn in bed while watching a movie since he was in college. Nathan was leaning on him and River was snoozing against Nathan's chest. The moment was picture perfect and one Charlie had thought would never happen. Then again, he'd never expected to have a family.

Now he couldn't imagine being without them.

His phone buzzed with an incoming message from Spencer.

You should check in with me first. Glad you're back. There's a meeting tomorrow with the assembly to discuss the details of your trip. Also, tomorrow you'll choose the format for the wedding. Will need you and Nathan to be there. Will also have you choose wedding rings.

Spencer could be so thorough. He sent back an answer.

Thanks.

Another text came through almost immediately.

Will you be in your office tonight?

He had to reply, but he didn't want to see Spencer until tomorrow.

Thanks for the update. Will be with Nathan and River tonight. Will see you in the morning.

When Spencer didn't reply right away, Charlie relaxed. He didn't want the royal interruptions tonight. Nathan needed him.

"When do you need to meet with Spencer?" Nathan asked. "Soon?"

"Want me to go?" Charlie kissed Nathan's head. "I thought I'd stick around tonight and not be the king for a little while."

"Really?" Nathan shifted to look him in the eye. "You're staying?"

"If we're going to live together once we're married, then we should start practicing living together." He wasn't sure how to balance family and work life, so this was a good way to learn. He rubbed Nathan's shoulder. "Is that fine with you?"

"It is." Hunger shimmered in his eyes. "I need to get River to bed. He should've been given a bath and he should be wearing his sleeper." Nathan eased one arm around River and managed to leave the bed with the baby in his embrace without waking him.

"I'm not sure what acrobatic move you just completed to do that, but I'm impressed." Charlie left the bed. "What can I do to help?"

"Turn the nightlight on and wind up the music box while I change him." Nathan carried the child to the cushioned table.

Charlie fumbled with the music box, but managed to make it work. The music lulled him, or maybe he was just that tired. Either way, he liked this domesticity.

Nathan changed River's diaper, then his outfit, and placed him in the crib. When he left the room, Nathan grasped Charlie's hand. "Now the hard part."

"Oh?" He followed Nathan out of the nursery. "How?"

"Because we have to be quiet and listen. He's a good sleeper, but he's cutting his second tooth and he'll wake easily. Then again, I don't rest all that well because I'm always listening for his movements or crying to go get him." Nathan left the nursery door partially open. "Now, where were we?"

Charlie gathered Nathan in his arms. "Right here." This was what he'd looked forward to for the last three days. The time apart had seemed like an eternity. He walked him to the bed.

Nathan eased onto the mattress and Charlie pushed him onto his back. Charlie craved this moment. He needed to be desired, but also to feel normal. Charlie kissed him, learning and tasting him. He breathed in the scent of Nathan, woodsy and sweet. Straddling him blew Charlie's mind. The man was so hard and lean. He couldn't wait to strip him and fully see his prize. Nathan was the best thing to happen to him.

He settled with Nathan on the bed and kissed him. Each taste and nibble kicked his desire up a few notches. He tangled with Nathan, needing to be one body. Yes, he and his lover had to be quiet, but that didn't mean they couldn't show each other pleasure. The springs squeaked with their every move, and when Nathan groaned, Charlie fought the urge to shush him.

He caressed Nathan's cock through the fabric of his jeans. Electricity bounced around his body. He marveled at the tenderness in Nathan's kiss. When Nathan bucked beneath him, Charlie unbuttoned and unzipped his jeans. He moved the denim and boxers down Nathan's thighs.

"Oh God," Nathan murmured. He yanked his shirt up, exposing his taut belly and chest. "More."

Charlie moved down Nathan's body to his cock. He removed his lover's pants and boxers, then fondled Nathan's sac. He admired the corded muscle of Nathan's belly and the way his nipples beaded. "Want you."

"Yes." Nathan writhed. "Touch me."

He would. He folded Nathan in half, admiring his ass. God, he had a nice butt. Full enough to swat, and sexy. He nipped along Nathan's inner thigh, then down to his cock. Nathan's skin reddened. His cock bobbed and he tensed.

Charlie couldn't wait any longer. He had to taste his lover. He sucked Nathan's dick into his mouth and basked in the saltiness. At the same time, he fondled Nathan's hole and sac.

Nathan groaned. He palmed Charlie's head, keeping him in place. When Charlie looked up at him, need filled Nathan's eyes. Desire radiated from him. Nathan bucked as Charlie bobbed his head.

"More, Charlie," Nathan murmured. He tensed. "Make love to me."

Soon. Charlie continued to lick and savor Nathan, but he also retrieved the small bottle of lube and condom he'd secreted in his pocket. Good thing he'd planned on making love tonight and come prepared. He lubed Nathan's asshole.

When Nathan whimpered, Charlie eased one finger into Nathan's body. He toyed with the puckered skin, but backed off long enough to speak. "Breathe," Charlie said. "Bear down and relax."

Nathan arched his back and groaned. He rammed his cock into Charlie's mouth as Charlie penetrated him. "Can't hold back." Nathan shuddered as the orgasm hit. He pushed deep into Charlie.

Cum slid down Charlie's throat and he loved it. He kept his finger in Nathan, prepping him as his lover relaxed. "Want me?" Charlie asked. "Right now?"

Nathan nodded and panted. His nipples beaded and his chest heaved.

"Need me?" Charlie asked as he pumped his digit into Nathan. He needed to strip. Right now, he wanted no barriers between them, save for the condom. "Tell me."

"Please?" Nathan bucked again. "Oh God."

He'd reduced Nathan to short sentences? *Good.* He wanted Nathan right on the edge, too. "I'm yours." He withdrew his finger and stripped. There was no time for finesse. The desire for Nathan was too strong. He sheathed himself and crawled onto the bed.

Nathan held on to his legs. When he smiled, the relaxation and beauty radiated from him. Charlie stroked himself, then lined his cock up with Nathan's hole. He pushed past the tight ring of muscle until he and Nathan were one body, complete together.

"So full," Nathan murmured.

He leaned over Nathan and stared into his eyes. He and Nathan had been made for each other. He belonged right here. Nathan whimpered, and the sound kickstarted Charlie's desire to move. He held on to Nathan's hips and began to thrust. He moved slowly at first. Within moments, he built into a steady rhythm and pushed with abandon.

Nathan met him thrust for thrust. The brown in his eyes deepened and ruddiness filled his cheeks. He reminded Charlie of a sculpture—so pretty and wonderful.

Charlie admired Nathan's body and the love between them. His moves turned feral in time with Nathan's and he pumped faster. He craved and adored this man. The sound of skin on skin and his moans seemed so loud in the room, despite his attempts to keep them quiet. Nothing else existed except Nathan.

Stars seemed to explode behind his eyelids and Charlie couldn't think straight. He gave in to the orgasm. Pleasure flooded his body. He wasn't sure how he was able to come without making much noise. He wanted to groan to show his thrill. He continued to thrust as the climax washed through them.

Nathan tensed and shuddered, then stilled. He held tight to Charlie's arms.

Charlie collapsed on him and kissed Nathan. His head swam, but he didn't care. He had everything he wanted in his arms.

Nathan broke the kiss. "Hold still."

He couldn't move if he tried.

"Shoot. River's awake," Nathan said. "He's still cutting that tooth." He nudged Charlie. "Sorry."

Charlie withdrew and flopped onto the bed. He'd have to get used to stealing moments with Nathan, but that wasn't so bad. Getting involved with a single father meant having to sacrifice here and there. He removed the condom and grabbed his boxer shorts from the floor. "Can I help?"

"Turn the music box back on, for one." Nathan donned a pair of shorts and fumbled into the nursery. He scooped River from the crib and cuddled him. "Can you get the teething ring from the fridge? Can't miss it."

"Sure." He finished winding the music box, then ventured through the suite to the kitchen area and retrieved the clear mushy plastic teething ring. He returned to the bedroom. "Here you go." He sat on the bed while Nathan rocked River.

Nathan closed his eyes as he soothed the child with the ring. "This is the hard part—well, one of them. I can't do much to help this. I can't make his teeth come through faster so it doesn't hurt any longer."

Charlie sat beside him. He rubbed River's back. He had so much to learn about kids. He'd thought he knew plenty from watching his sister raise Alistair, but he'd been wrong. Watching wasn't the same as experiencing. "I feel helpless, too. I don't know what to do in general."

"It's a balancing act." Nathan bumped shoulders with him. "This is what I meant when I asked if you'd still want to be with me. It's not easy."

"No." He hadn't planned on switching from hot sex to soothing a baby this fast, but this wouldn't be any different if River was his own child.

"There we go. Rest, big guy." Nathan continued to soothe River. He sighed. "Almost there."

Charlie watched Nathan as he carried the baby back to the nursery. When Nathan returned a few moments later without River, he walked straight to the bed and collapsed.

"He's asleep." Nathan buried his face in the pillows for a second, then turned his head. "I have to lean on Mrs. Major so much, but I can't expect her to take care of him without my help. He's my responsibility."

"It's understandable." Charlie stretched out beside him. "Is this how it will always be? Weird interruptions and stolen moments?"

Nathan rolled onto his side and the muscle in his jaw tightened. "It could. I have a son and he needs attention. I can't shirk it all onto the nanny."

"I know." He sounded so jealous. He'd end up leaving Nathan behind a lot because of his role. The king had duties he couldn't drag friends along for and Nathan would have to adjust. He scooted closer to Nathan and held him. "I'm sorry I sounded like a dick. I get how jealous I look and it's not attractive. I've never had to share my affections with someone, but I can't imagine sharing them with anyone else."

Nathan laced his fingers with Charlie's and stared at him in the dim light. "Are you having second thoughts? It's not too late." His voice cracked. "Being with me is difficult because River and I are a pair."

"I know." He dragged the blanket over them and held Nathan. "This whole thing has gotten out of control. It's harder than I ever thought it'd be, but it's exactly what I want. I want to be with someone who is strong and can handle my life, but also someone who will challenge me. I look at things differently because I have to consider you and River. That's made me more compassionate."

Nathan closed his eyes. "And the stuff with my mother?"

"Doesn't bother me," Charlie said. "I've got all sorts of people who come out of the woodwork wanting things from me. They think because I looked at them or spoke to them for a second, I owe them. I'm used to it. But you're different. You haven't asked anything from me besides love and commitment. I can't wait for Christmas Eve so we can be married and cement this life we've got going. You're the one for me."

Nathan snuggled closer to him. "You're mine, too."

"Sleep. I'll be here when you wake up and I'll help you with River. We're a team." Let trouble come their way. He didn't care. He had Nathan and River. Life was good.

* * * *

The next morning, Charlie surfaced from sleep and clung to Nathan. He'd spent the better part of the night up and down with River and Nathan. It hadn't been the most restful evening, yet he'd never been so refreshed and happy. He liked the family situation. Some might say he was playing house, and he'd quickly disagree. This wasn't playing. He cared about River and wanted to see him grow up. He'd fallen for Nathan, too.

He wanted a future with them. The fake engagement had become quite real.

His phone rang. "Shit. Must be Spencer," he muttered and let go of Nathan. He fumbled on the nightstand for his phone and hoped he hadn't woken either Nathan or River up.

"Hello?" He left the bed and crept over to the far end of the room. "Spencer?"

"We have a problem," Spencer said. "You need to come to the office alone."

"Why? What's gone haywire?" He groaned. "Talk to me."

"I'd rather tell you in person," Spencer said. "The *Royal Rag* got a hold of the story about you and Nathan's engagement being fake. Someone spilled the story."

"Well, that's easy. It's not. We're a team and you can print that. I can't wait to marry him." He'd never been more confident in his life.

"I know that, you know that and everyone connected to the family does, but the public isn't convinced."

"Understood." He wasn't sure how to make it any clearer, though. "How do you suggest we make this more believable?"

"How about a public event with him in attendance?" Spencer asked. "My guess is a royal reception, maybe a party for kids or something the people of the kingdom can attend and enjoy."

"Plan a Christmas party, then." He watched Nathan sleep. Such a pretty man in slumber, and god knew Nathan could use a few more hours of ZZs. "Plan the party for the twentieth. That gives us, what, ten days to plan it?"

"Nine, but yes," Spencer said. "There's more."

"What?" Christ. He didn't have time for this.

"There are photos. Look, just come to your office."

"What photos?" He needed to get dressed. "Just tell me."

Spencer sighed. "There are photos of Nathan and his ex-boyfriend that surfaced. They show him kissing this man, a Mack Dallas. According to Dallas, he's still dating Nathan."

"That's garbage." He knew Nathan. "Let me guess, for a price, the man will can the story? He'll go away if we give him money?"

"You've got it."

"Tough shit." He tucked the phone between his ear and his shoulder as he pulled on his trousers. "I'll be right there." Some days it sucked to be the king.

"Get dressed," Spencer said.

"I will." He hung up and focused on finding his shirt. He should be discussing the situation with Nathan, too, not hiding it from him.

Nathan sat up, bleary-eyed. "What's going on?" He scrubbed both hands over his face. "Is River up?"

"No." He donned his socks and shoes. Where was his shirt?

"Is everything all right?" Nathan left the bed. "You're tense. Charlie?"

Charlie picked up his shirt. He wanted to scream, but this wasn't the place and Nathan hadn't done anything wrong.

"Charlie?" Nathan shrank away from him. "What'd I do?"

"I'm not sure." He had to get himself under control. He knew Nathan. Cheating wasn't his style. That didn't mean having someone try to sabotage what they'd created didn't hurt. "I don't have the entire story, but a man named Mack Dallas claims he's in a relationship with you."

Nathan paled. "Oh God."

"My gut says you're not lying, but I need the whole truth." He curled his fingers under Nathan's chin to center himself and gain strength. "Please?"

Nathan cleared his throat. "To be totally honest, I'm only in a relationship with you. I broke up with Mack eight months ago. River wasn't born yet and we split because he wanted to be a social butterfly. I wanted to be a dad and our plans didn't mesh, simple as that."

"And the photos of you together? He released them last night." He cupped Nathan's cheek. "He wants money."

"Don't pay him. Those photos are old. Have to be. I've been here since River was born."

"That's what I thought." Charlie texted Spencer, summoning him to the suite. "Then let's get this dealt with."

"Let me get dressed and check on River." Nathan switched into a pair of jeans and a T-shirt, then left the room.

Charlie folded his jacket and wished he could've been doing anything else instead of persecuting Nathan. He trusted this man, but the photos had rocked him and he hadn't even seen them yet. He didn't like the idea of Nathan being with someone else.

He spotted Nathan's phone. If Nathan were doing something other than taking care of his son, then he'd have his phone.

Nathan returned a moment later. "Your sister is here. She and Mrs. Major are taking the boys to play. Spencer just showed up, too."

"Good." He tossed the jacket onto the bed. "Let's get this over with."

Spencer joined them in the bedroom. He held a thick folder and a laptop. "Hi, Nathan. Charlie, your sister and Mrs. Major are leaving."

"Fine." Charlie stood. "Where are these photos?"

Spencer opened the folder. "They're online, but I've printed them." He spread the images out on the bed. "These."

Charlie gazed at the images. None of them were particularly damning, especially since the photos appeared to have been taken in the summer — long before he'd started the relationship with Nathan. If they photos had been taken recently, then they hadn't been done anywhere in Lysianna.

"That's Cleveland." Nathan pointed to one photo. "That's from the weekend we visited my college alma mater, and that's Public Square. Those are four years old at least, because they haven't had traffic on that part of Public Square in at least that long and there are cars behind us."

Spencer nodded. "We've traced the images. None have been taken in this country and there is no proof Nathan has left the royal estate since May."

"Because I haven't," Nathan said. "I've been here."

Charlie eyed his lover. If Nathan was hiding anything, he was doing a good job. "Okay, then how much does this guy want? Or shall I ask, what does he want?"

"Half a million," Spencer said. "He claims he's got damning proof he and Nathan were together last night."

"I can attest to that being bunk," Charlie said. "We were here with the baby."

Nathan shook his head. "I should've known this would happen. Should've guessed this."

"Guessed what?" Charlie asked. Nathan's statements pricked Charlie's interest. "Nathan?"

"I should've expected Mack and everyone else from my past would try something. They see there might be a chance they can get something out of this and they're trying." Nathan continued to shake his head. "People want to be close to you because you're the king and think I can do that for them."

"Slow down." Charlie embraced Nathan. "People will come out of the woodwork, you're right, but that doesn't mean we have to acknowledge them."

"I'm sorry." Nathan shuddered. "I got wrapped up in you and forgot my common sense."

"It's okay." Charlie gestured to Spencer. "We know those are just ploys to get money and fame. Kindly let this jerk know we're not paying anything and thank you for the effort...something like that."

"Yes, my king." Spencer gathered the images into the folder. "There is more, though."

"What?" Nathan wobbled. "I haven't done anything."

Charlie held on to Nathan and petted his hair. "What more? What's going on?"

"Lender has surfaced." Spencer opened the laptop and pointed to images on the internet. "He released these."

Charlie kept Nathan in his embrace and looked at the photos. He'd seen this tactic before. "Telephoto...blurry...what am I seeing?"

"Charlie, it's Lender and Nathan. That's Nathan." Spencer pointed to the screen. "He says he collaborated with Nathan to get you to marry him so he can dump you at the last minute. This is all an elaborate ploy to dupe you."

Charlie sighed and held on to Nathan's shoulder. "Nathan?"

"That's not what happened at all. That's the day he threatened me." Nathan shivered. He rubbed his bare arms. "I was on my way to work after you told me you were the king. I was angry, but when I got to the archives, I decided to go back home. When I went back across the commons, Lender stopped me. He kept pulling me close and I tried to pull away. It felt wrong. Then he threatened me. That's when I went back to the archives and called you. I never agreed to anything he said. Charlie, I'm scared of Lender."

"It does seem rather coincidental that you needed help that got you to living in the castle." Spencer stepped away from the laptop. "Once you learned who he was, you suddenly needed protection?"

"No." Nathan shook his head again. "It's not like that."

Charlie watched Nathan. He'd never been good at judging the character of his boyfriends, but Nathan was different. He'd been so up front with Charlie. Still, the story annoyed Charlie. How could someone concoct a lie this awful?

"Charlie?" Nathan's shoulders sank. "You don't believe me."

"I never said that." Charlie scrubbed the back of his neck with his palm. He had to think this through. "I'm confused."

Spencer shut the laptop. "What are you going to do?"

He still didn't have an idea, but he had to decide. "I'm going to send you to the office. I'll be there in a few minutes. Start planning the party for the children of the kingdom. I want that to go on. Understood? Thank you, Lord Spencer." He dismissed his advisor.

Nathan sank onto the bed. He covered his face with his hands and Charlie waited for Spencer to leave before they spoke. He'd never seen a more dejected man in his life.

Once Spencer was gone, Charlie knelt between Nathan's knees. "Hey."

Nathan brushed the back of his hand across his mouth. "Hi. When do you want me to leave?"

"Whoa. Slow down." Charlie grasped Nathan's hands. "No one said anything about going."

"Things are a mess. We had a whole eight days together and we've got a disaster. You need focus and to be a leader, not dealing with this intrusion." Nathan massaged his forehead. "You should be running the country, not running interference for me."

Nathan had a point, not that Charlie wanted to argue.

"So I'll go." Nathan tried to leave the bed. "Charlie."

"Being with me is messy business. It doesn't always work out right," Charlie said. He brushed tears from Nathan's cheeks. "Do you love Mack?"

"No. I'm not sure I ever really did."

He hadn't thought so. "What about Lender? There is no possibility he's telling the truth, is there?"

"He demanded I leave you alone and I said, sure, yeah, I'll do that, but I never meant it. I was trying to get the hell away from him," Nathan said. "I didn't know you well at that time, but I felt the spark between us already. There was no leaving you alone, but when he threatened to hurt River..."

"Did you agree to leave me? Even if it was said in jest or a way to shake him?"

"I agreed to leave you alone to get him to do the same to me. I never made a deal with him." Nathan looked him in the eye. "I'd never met him before and wanted to get away from him. The only one I've ever gotten into an agreement with is you."

He thought so. Nathan had appeared scared in those photos, not like a man who'd just made a deal. "Okay."

Nathan balled his hands on his lap, but said nothing.

"Then we need to do something." Charlie stood. "As far as Lender knows, he's got the upper hand. He thinks he's punishing me, but he's not. All he's doing is stoking my anger." He paced the length of the room. "I'm spending my time dealing with this and not the country. He knows how to play the game and thinks he's spreading my attention too thin."

"Charlie."

He smiled, knowing full well what he wanted to do. "We're going to play him in return."

"We are?" Nathan remained seated. "How?"

"Easy. I'm putting the rumor out there that we're already married." Charlie's smile widened. "Yes, we'll take a wedding photo and send it out to the world. That'll teach him." It might not be the real wedding picture, but that wouldn't matter once they did get married in due time.

"That won't change anything."

"It will." Charlie stopped pacing. "You're going to be there when he confronts me and we'll figure it out. Maybe you can confront him and tell him you've done what he asks. That way it'll be on the cameras and we'll nail him."

"Charlie."

"It's going to work." Charlie tugged Nathan to his feet and embraced him. "When it's all over, you can decide for yourself if you want to marry me. No pressure." It all made sense.

"I already know." Nathan flattened his hands on Charlie's chest. "I don't need to extort him or whatever."

"Then we'll have to put our heads together to come up with something better." Charlie kissed him. "Either way, we'll get him."

"Charlie, wait." Nathan balled his hands. "I can't lie. I'm not good at it and never have been."

"We need to get rid of Lender and I'm not forcing you to marry me right now." He couldn't do that to Nathan. "You have to do this of your own free will."

Nathan leaned back in his arms, but pain resonated in his eyes. "What if we have a small ceremony — something informal, but legal and with witnesses? Just enough for the marriage to be legal and you to keep your crown? We'll know it happened and so will your sister, but he can think it's not happened yet," he said. "No one will be lying that way."

"The people will expect a big wedding." Charlie couldn't disappoint the people.

"So we do it big on Christmas Eve." Nathan disengaged from him. "As long as you have proof and witnesses that we're married, you'll be fine. The crown will be yours."

Charlie paused. He was about to get everything he wanted, but the victory felt hollow. "Wait."

Nathan faced him. "What? I've thought it all out. You can get a minister, your family, the kids and Spencer along with Mrs. Major rounded up and we'll marry so you can be king. Problem solved."

"Is that what you truly want?"

"To help you?" Nathan asked. "Yes."

"I don't do divorces." Once he married Nathan, that was it.

"Who says you need to?" Nathan shrugged. "You get what you want, he's stopped and everyone's happy."

"Except you." He could see it in Nathan's eyes — this wasn't what he'd bargained for.

"Sure." The light didn't reach his eyes and he didn't smile or embrace Charlie. "I am."

Why was he trying so hard to act happy all while looking miserable? "Nathan? I thought you wanted to marry me. Thought you were okay with being beside, but sort of behind me, too. Did you change your mind This was the plan—I get the crown and you're protected." *What am I doing wrong?*

Nathan said nothing and left him alone in the bedroom. Charlie sank onto the bed. Something wasn't right and he didn't get it. He'd thought they loved each other and the wedding would be easy.

He had to get his act together. Charlie left the suite, only to run into Spencer in the corridor.

"What happened? He looked miserable." Spencer fell into step with him.

"I know this much. He was with Mack, but not for most of the year and they aren't a couple. He was pushed into those photos with Lender and inadvertently agreed to lie to me because he thought it'd get him away from Lender." He stuffed his hands into his pockets. "As for the wedding, he's still agreed to marry me, but for a man about to wed a king, he looked heartsick. So, yeah, life is just peachy."

"I thought you were already getting married," Spencer said.

"Right."

"I missed something." Spencer stopped short. "Why is he upset?"

"I'm not sure, and trust me, I wish I knew." He shook his head. "One minute, things are great. We're together and things are fine. Then the next minute, he looks like I've taken away his birthday. I guess I missed something, too."

Spencer stayed rooted to the spot. "Did you tell him how you feel? Or did you just sort of steamroll over him with your plans?"

"What?" A dull throb started behind his eyes. "What do you mean?"

"Do you love him?"

"Of course. I'm marrying him, aren't I? It's expected."

Spencer groaned. "I get it."

"You do?" He pinched the bridge of his nose. "Then tell me."

"Remember how Princess Angel and Prince John were pushed together? Remember how she looked at him? She loved him to his core and he could do no wrong in her eyes because he was the one."

"I remember." The wedding had seemed to take too long and had bored him to tears.

"Remember how John sort of brushed her off? He said he loved her and never showed it," Spencer said. "He went through the motions with her."

"It happens. Running a country is hard work." He'd never thought Angel and John had been a good fit, but he hadn't been the one playing matchmaker. "So?"

"You don't see it. Nathan fell for you. He doesn't need the theatrics or the threat of Lender hanging over his head to know he wants to be with you. He absolutely loves you."

"He hasn't told me that." He would've remembered Nathan saying such things.

"Don't be dense. A man doesn't introduce you to his child, tell you his problems and bend over backwards for you out of duty. He's doing it for love," Spencer said. "Do you get it? He loves you — the real you."

"You bend over backwards for me and it's very much out of duty."

"But I'm not in love with you," Spencer snapped. "He is."

Charlie stared at his advisor. *Shit.* The lines about getting the family together, something small and being legal weren't smokescreens or anything else. Nathan had been honest with him. "I get it." But he didn't know what to do.

"Then don't half-ass this." Spencer groaned and shook his head again. "Permit me to be blunt a bit longer. Do you want to marry him because you love him or because it's what you feel you have to do?"

"I love him."

"Then stop looking at this as a business transaction or something you have to do because of that decree, and put your heart in it. Do what you want because you love him. Sure, the window for this to work is tight, but that doesn't mean shit if you care about him and can't let him go," Spencer said.

He could be dense, like Spencer mentioned, but he understood. The games were over. His man, the one he'd waited and searched for, was here. If he wanted him, then he'd have to marry him.

Now.

"Spencer? Get the family together — whoever's here. I want Mrs. Major, Ren and you. I'm going to marry Nathan tonight because I can't see my life without him. Fuck the decree."

"There's the Charlie I know and love as a friend." Spencer shook hands with him. "Give me an hour. I'm assuming you want him dressed up, though."

"Yes—but only if you can talk him into it." He winked. "I'm off to get the royal minister." He knew what he had to do and how he wanted to show Nathan he loved him.

"Now you're taking." Spencer sped away.

Charlie grinned to himself. He might be under pressure and royally fucking up the wedding details, but he had the most important detail in mind—he'd marry the man he loved tonight.

Now all he had to do was convince Nathan the love they shared was real.

Chapter Eleven

Nathan stood at the edge of the royal nursery and watched his son play. He tried not to let his romantic life get in the way of his time with River. Today, he couldn't help himself.

He'd thought he'd shown Charlie how much he cared. Thought he'd proven he just wanted to be with him. That he loved him.

All Charlie cared about was defeating Lender. Did the damn decree matter that much?

"You look destroyed." Zara hugged him. "My brother said something, didn't he?"

"He's doing his duty. I just have to adjust." He sighed to compose himself. "It's okay. I know the score now."

She lowered her voice. "What did he say?"

"We get married, put Lender in his place then figure things out." In hindsight, the plan wasn't so crappy, but in the moment it had seemed downright cruel.

"But? You're upset, so there must be more to the story."

"I thought he understood I love him. He sees the wedding as a duty and I don't want to marry him out of duty," Nathan said. "It's not right."

"No, it's not." She hugged him. "But I know my brother, and while he might have his foot wedged in his mouth, I know he loves you, too. Do you trust me?"

"Do I have a choice? I love him and I don't want this to end, but I refuse to be his husband in name only." His voice cracked and his emotions held by a thread.

"Then trust me." She steered him toward the door. "Mrs. Major and I have the boys in order. I want you to go to the royal spa—yes, we have one—and relax. There's a royal reception tonight. Black tie and tuxedo thing. Charlie's dealing with a contract issue right now or he'd have told you himself and he can't do spa time with you. But Luke can."

"This seems odd." He'd rather stay in tonight. "I should be with River."

"I told you to trust me, didn't I? This reception requires you to be there." She grasped his shoulders. "Would I steer you wrong?"

"I'm not in the mood for these games. I want to go home." God, he hated admitting defeat, but the sheer weight of the situation crushed him. "Don't you get it?"

"I do." She dragged him into the hallway. "This is important and I know you're tired. I know he hurt your heart, too. He's hard to handle, but this is the way it is when you're with the king. You're stronger than you think and you can handle this. It's a dinner and reception. You'll have to deal with these for the rest of your life and it's not a big deal. Charlie needs you and you love him, right?"

"Yes." He couldn't argue with her there.

"Then show up. Be the support he needs. He leans on you for a lot and neither of you realize it. Why? Because you're not fawning over him like most people and you're not puffing his ego. You're the balance he craves."

She made sense. Besides, he didn't want to give up on Charlie. "Okay."

"And Luke is dying to have a guy to chat with." She smiled and hugged him. "Poor Luke. He can't wait until Alli is big enough to do guy stuff. I'm too much glitter and pink sparkles for him. He wants to watch the big game and talk about baseball. I've seen baseball and it's not that exciting."

"I see." Her comment broke the tension and helped changed Nathan's mind. "I'll do it."

"Good. Oh, and you'll like the reception. It's not as bad as you think it will be." She held up one hand. "And, I'll make sure River and Mrs. Major are taken care of, okay?"

"Deal." He shook his head. "Where is Luke?"

"Right here." Luke ventured up to him. "Ready?"

"Sure." He couldn't miss the twinkle in Luke's eye or the way Zara grinned. Something didn't quite gel here, but he wasn't sure what.

Luke closed the nursery door. "I love my wife dearly, but her enthusiasm will be the death of me. My house is full of sparkly stuff, and she's right—I want to watch a baseball game with someone who isn't asking a hundred questions or getting bored by the third inning."

"I played baseball for four years in junior high and high school," Nathan said. "I liked the camaraderie of the team."

"Nice." Luke walked with him down the corridor to a glass wall. "This is the spa. I like the haircuts and shaves you get here. It's nice to have a straight razor shave every so often."

"I've never had one before." He followed him into the spa.

"What position did you play?" Luke asked and nodded to the barber. "Hi, Rick."

"I was a short stop." Nathan stayed next to Luke. "What do we do?"

"I played first base, but I loved painting more, so I quit my freshman year." He pointed to the stylist chairs. "Tell Rick what you want in your cut and shave and he'll do it."

He'd never been treated this way. "All I need is a trim. Nothing drastic."

"Then tell them." Luke sat beside him.

Nathan allowed the barber to trim his hair and opted for the straight razor shave. It was nice to have the hot lather before and the towel after the shave. Having such an indulgence wasn't something he wanted to do often, but it was nice.

An hour later, he stepped out of the dressing room. "I've never had anyone work so hard to fit me into a tuxedo." Then again, he'd never needed to wear a tux before.

"Oh yeah, these things are too constricting for me, but Zara likes the way I look in them." Luke adjusted his cummerbund. "You look great."

"Do we meet up with them somewhere?" He'd like to see Charlie for a moment before and apologize for being frustrated.

"We'll catch them in the reception room. It's just outside the ballroom. This way." Luke strode down the dark corridor, but stopped short. "Actually, I could swear Zara said something about the flowers being in here."

"Sure." He was just along for the ride. "I still get lost in the castle."

"It's been a year and I get lost, too." Luke pointed to a hallway to the left. "Okay, so we go this way."

"Do you go to these receptions often?" Nathan asked.

"Not as much as we could. Charlie holds a lot fewer of them, I'm told. I guess their father had receptions for almost everything."

He continued down the corridor with Luke. Since he had a moment, he had questions. "Did you get any help when you joined the family? I mean, did they tell you what to do and how to act? I don't know if I'm wearing the right things or if I'm following the rules, because no one told me if there are rules."

Luke stopped outside the chapel. "I know. They sort of forget that people who aren't born into the family or this lifestyle have no idea how to act accordingly. They've always lived this way, so it's strange to them to think otherwise. In my case, I made mistakes, but Zara gave me a hand. Charlie will help you, too."

"Do you think so?"

"I know so. I got thrown into the thick of things without a net, so I know where you're coming from." Luke dipped his head. "Here come the flowers."

When Nathan turned, Charlie approached. He held a boutonniere of roses and holly. "Hi."

"Hi." Nathan wanted to launch himself into Charlie's arms, but held back. "You're pinning the flowers on me?"

"I am." Charlie affixed the roses to Nathan's lapel. "You look sexy."

"Thank you." He stepped back to admire Charlie. "You look all royal and stuff. I like it."

"Good," Charlie said. "We need to talk."

"We can talk later. I don't want you to be late for this reception." He forced a smile. "This is more important."

"Actually, you're more important." Charlie bridged the gap between them. "You being here is crucial to me and I would be lost without you."

"Even after a week?"

"Yes."

He appreciated the lack of hesitation in Charlie's answer. It reassured him a bit.

"I need you to understand something." Charlie held Nathan's hands. "I need to get married to retain the crown, but I need you to be my husband because you're part of my team. You're the one who balances me."

"I try." Part of the team? It made him sound like an assistant. Nathan stared into Charlie's eyes. He loved the earnestness there in the blue depths. "What do you want from me?"

"I want to be married to you because I need you. I need the strong presence you give me," Charlie said. "I want to be your husband because I love you, but I'm scared."

"Of what?" *He loves me!* What was he afraid of? "Of me?"

"That you'll change your mind. This is a crazy life. People don't like the fishbowl I live in and I'm worried you'll take the best things to happen to me and leave because it's too hard."

"I can't guarantee I'll never leave you because I can't guarantee I won't die before you, but I can guarantee you have my heart." He kissed Charlie. "I'm yours."

"Good." Charlie relaxed a little. "Now, this reception isn't for everyone, or even the heads of state."

"No? What is it for?"

"Us."

He frowned. "Huh?" This didn't make sense.

"Us. I don't want to lose the crown, but I can't lose you. The minister is there and he's ready to marry us. My family, Mrs. Major and River are in there, too. It's the small wedding you want. Will you do me the honor of being my husband?" Charlie's hands trembled. "This way, we're legal and we have time to fall deeper in love."

"Charlie?" He couldn't believe his ears.

"I love you and want you as my husband. I can't imagine being with anyone else." The muscle in Charlie's jaw tightened. "I love you more than I ever thought possible, and last night proved to me that you're what I want. I can't see my life without you."

Nathan's knees wobbled. Charlie was saying the right things. He wanted to marry Charlie and begin their life together. They'd have bumps, but he trusted they could handle it if they worked together.

"Well? Will you go in there with me and marry me?" Charlie asked.

"I will." He couldn't imagine being with anyone else, either. "Let's go get married."

"God, I love you." Charlie held Nathan's hand. "We will be expected to have a bigger wedding on Christmas Eve, but this ensures we're legal."

"And if something goes wrong on Christmas Eve, we're covered?" Charlie's plan was smart.

"That, and I want to make love to my husband," Charlie said. "Tonight."

"Yes." Nathan couldn't get into the chapel and married to Charlie fast enough. He had a partner, a lover and a wonderful man he refused to let go.

* * * *

"I now pronounce you husband and husband," the royal minister said. "You may kiss your husband."

Charlie kissed Nathan. They'd done it—gotten married. *Holy shit*. No more lying or hiding. When Nathan smiled and looked into Charlie's eyes, he knew to his soul he'd made the right choice.

"Does this make you legal?" Zara asked. "Tell me it does."

Nathan held Charlie's hand, but scooped River into his free arm.

"Unless Father comes back and says something isn't right, then this is legal." Charlie kissed River on the top of the head. "I've got my family around me—all of it."

"Where is Father?" Zara asked. "Didn't he want to be here?"

"He's coming in for the Christmas Eve festivities." Charlie slid his arm around Nathan. "I'll have Spencer contact him again to get him to come home faster, but it's a diplomatic mission—or so he says." He shrugged.

Luke hugged Nathan, then Charlie. "Question. If I've been made a prince and Alistair is a prince...so what does that make Nathan? What does it make River? They should be princes or something."

"I'm not a prince or prince material." Nathan blushed. "I'm his husband."

"It's true. You're married to a king, but that also makes you officially a royal," Zara said. "Charlie?"

"We'll discuss it later." He wasn't sure what title Nathan should be given. Luke had been made a prince, but Charlie wasn't even sure there were protocols for a commoner marrying a king.

Mrs. Major ventured over. "Nathan, I'm proud of you. This is where you belong. I'm happy for you both." She hugged Charlie. "My king."

"You'll be staying on as nanny, yes?" Charlie hugged her. "You've served us well."

"I would be honored." She bowed. "Thank you, my king."

Charlie let go of her and rubbed Nathan's back. "We need to sign the official document."

"Oh." Nathan shifted River to his other arm and followed Charlie to the dais. The minister offered them a fountain pen. Zara and Luke stood to Charlie's right, while Spencer and Mrs. Major were on Nathan's left to witness the signing.

Charlie scrawled his name on the document and his heart hammered as he waited for Nathan to do the same. "Let me take him." He scooped River into his arms. "Hi."

River squirmed, then tugged at Charlie's lapel. He pulled at the petals on the rose.

Nathan signed his name. "I guess we're legal." He glanced over his shoulder. "River, you can't destroy that."

Charlie batted Nathan away. "He can't hurt anything. It's just a couple of petals."

"The pin." Nathan removed the boutonniere. "There."

Charlie snorted. He hadn't thought about the pin and the chance River could injure himself. Boy, did he have a lot to learn. "Sorry."

"You'll figure it out." Nathan held the flowers. "I'm still learning. Once I think I know how to handle something, he throws something new at me. Teething comes to mind."

"I guess so." He'd never forget trying to sleep while Nathan soothed the poor kid. He'd offered to take turns, but when he'd rocked River, the child hadn't settled. Only Nathan had the right touch.

"Okay, everyone. Family photo." Zara waved. "Father Kaplan, you too. We need to commemorate this event. Mrs. Major? You as well. Come on, Spencer."

Charlie held River and tucked Nathan to his side. He wanted lots of photos. This was the biggest moment of his life. He smiled while Zara set up the camera.

He couldn't wait to start his life with River and Nathan.

"I'm doing this one on the timer," she said and hustled over to the group. "Then Luke can take the rest."

Once the photo session concluded, Charlie stood in front of everyone. "Thank you for sharing this rather hastily created event with us. It means so much to Nathan, River and me."

Nathan knelt with River and allowed the baby to stand, even though River was wobbly.

"We will be having a bigger event on Christmas Eve, one the people of Lysianna can attend and enjoy." Charlie applauded. "But right now, we should put a little boy to bed."

Nathan nodded. "Thank you, everyone."

"Put him to bed? Or so you can enjoy and celebrate your wedding?" Zara asked and waggled her eyebrows. "We know what you're going to do."

Nathan blushed and averted his gaze.

"You should decide what title you're giving Nathan, too," Luke said. "After other important things."

"It's on the list." Charlie helped Nathan to his feet and took River from him. "If you need us, go through Spencer, but don't need us." Hopefully, they'd have peace and quiet for the night.

Luke winked. "Enjoy and good luck."

Charlie waved, then grasped Nathan's hand. He didn't speak until they were alone in the corridor. "Did I surprise you?"

"You did." Nathan walked with him. "I didn't believe you'd tell me you loved me."

"Why?" He patted River's bottom in time with their footsteps.

"Because you're the king and could have anyone. You could be with another dignitary or one of your other boyfriends, instead of me. I'm plain." Nathan hooked his fingers in Charlie's pocket. "And it's been so fast. I was afraid you'd find someone while you were away and realize you could do better, or that you'd come to your senses that you should be with a wealthy man. Someone who can handle your social set."

"You're just what I want." He made his way down to the guest suite. "I worried you'd realize being with me is difficult and change your mind. You'd want to be with someone who wasn't gone so much." He stopped at their door and opened it. "You also could do better than me."

"How?"

"Because you could be with someone who has a regular job and knows about kids." He carried River to the nursery. "I'm impressed someone found a small enough tuxedo for him."

"Zara provided that. She said it was Alistair's for some party." Nathan left his jacket on the chair and rolled up his sleeves. He removed River's jacket and pants. "He'll need changing and to have a bottle. I'll change him if you get the bottle. I believe there's one made up in the fridge. Just warm it up a little." He set about changing the child's clothes and diaper.

Charlie ditched his jacket in the living room and went to the kitchen area. He'd seen Zara get bottles for Alistair. He could handle this, right? It couldn't be too hard to make up a bottle. He searched the fridge for the item, but unless he was mistaken, there wasn't anything made up.

Nathan carried River into the kitchen. "What's wrong?"

"I can't find the bottle." He felt silly. He should be able to locate one. "What do I do?"

"You get it out of the cupboard here." He bounced River on his hip. "Here. Fill this with water to the ten-ounce line and I'll get the formula. I have already boiled water in the fridge—just pop it in the microwave for twenty seconds at a time until it's room temperature. Wash your hands while the water heats."

"Oh." Charlie found the container and did as he'd been told until the water was up to temp. He washed his hands, then filled the bottle. "Now what?"

"This." Nathan brought over the container of powder. "Add two scoops of this, then put the nipple and lid combination on it. Shake the bottle, but make sure the lid is on tight or you'll have a mess."

"Got it." He did as told. After helping Nathan, Charlie appreciated what Zara did a whole lot more. Being a parent was so complicated. It was a good thing he didn't mind learning on the job. "Here."

"Good." Nathan accepted the bottle. "If you want to change, go ahead. I'll be in the nursery feeding him."

"I don't have much to change." Charlie unhooked his cufflinks, then unbuttoned his shirt. He left the tie on the bed. While Nathan fed River, Charlie removed his phone from his pocket and placed the device on the nightstand. A thought occurred to him. He hadn't chosen a ring for Nathan. *Shit.* He should wear one since they were now married. He sank onto the bed. There were so many details he'd forgotten — rings, for one.

Nathan wandered into the bedroom. He had a towel on his shoulder and was patting River's bottom. "He's fighting sleep."

"Of course." There had been too much going on and Charlie wanted to be alone with Nathan. The baby could sense the need and innately knew to interrupt it. Charlie wished Mrs. Major were there, but she deserved some time off. "We'll figure out how to make it work."

"I'll bet you never thought you'd say that, did you?" Nathan kept pacing. "He'll wear out in a bit."

"I'm sure." Charlie shrugged out of his shirt. "I've said a lot of things I never thought I'd say. Never thought I'd get married, never thought I'd marry a man with a kid or that I'd be given the honor of helping to raise the kid. But being a king and being in love with you means I get to do a lot of things that are new, which makes me happy. But being married also reminds me that I didn't give you a wedding ring."

"You gave me this one." Nathan wiggled his fingers. "This is enough, and by rights, I should've picked a ring out for you."

"I suppose you're right, but what if you don't want to wear that one? Or you want something simple for when you're in the archives working?" Charlie removed his watch. "We never did sort out the wedding details. I guess we should've."

"You've got the details for the ball done. What do we need to add? To reserve the chapel? To get dresses or tuxedoes for the wedding party? Who is in the wedding party? You've got flowers for the ball. We can use those," Nathan said. "But we also have time to decide this stuff. We don't have to conquer the world tonight."

"True enough. I'd like my sister to stand with us, and Luke. Who do you want?" Charlie asked. "Do you want anyone, or will Luke do?"

"I'm happy with your brother-in-law." Nathan stopped walking. "Just a moment. Will you wind the music box?"

"Sure." Now this was something he could handle. He turned the key on the box, starting the soft music.

Nathan placed River in the crib. He stood next to the child's bed for a moment, then tiptoed out of the room.

"Are we good?" Charlie whispered. "Will he sleep?"

"He's crashed. There was enough action today, but the teething ring is chilling just in case." Nathan cracked the door to the nursery and sighed. "Okay. Wow. Who knew getting married would take so much out of me?"

"A surprise wedding is taxing." Charlie grasped Nathan's hands and directed him to the bed. "We're legal and alone."

"We are." Nathan collapsed underneath him on the mattress. "Having a child takes it out of you, too."

"I don't know how you do it." He tangled up with Nathan and stared into his eyes. Now he'd have the rest of his life to enjoy his husband. He marveled at those words a moment. *My husband.* God, he was a lucky man. "I love you, Nathan Pratt."

"I love you, too." Nathan kissed him. "I like seeing you naked, too."

"Just a moment." He couldn't strip fast enough. He left the bed and removed his pants and socks. When he turned back to the bed, his phone rang. "You're kidding me."

"Answer it," Nathan said. "Could be important."

Honestly, he doubted that. He picked up the phone. Spencer's name filled the ID portion of the screen. "This had better be urgent," he said. He wasn't in the mood to deal with anyone except Nathan. "Spencer."

Spencer answered right away. "Charlie, we've got problems."

Chapter Twelve

Charlie bit back a groan and paced the room. "You've got to be kidding me." *A problem. Just what I need.* "What is it?"

"Lender found out about the wedding and he got your former stepmother involved," Spencer said. "She can't do anything about the wedding, but she claims that since your father didn't witness the nuptials, it's not enough to satisfy the decree."

"What?" He massaged his temples. "Spencer. Since when was that in the decree?" He should've read it more thoroughly.

"Since it was in the fine print," Spencer said. "I went through the document and the wording is there."

"How in the hell do I convince my father to come back now? He's busy on his diplomatic trip," Charlie said. Everything was so out of control again.

"You do realize he met a woman in the States and is with her, right? The diplomacy has been to convince her to come to Lysianna." Spencer sighed. "I'll try to contact him, but I'd suggest you do, too. You might be able to get him to pick up the phone."

"I will in the morning. It's only the eleventh and we've got some time." He paused. "There isn't a built-in provision saying I have to have Dad handle this within a certain time period, is there? Meaning, as long as we show we're married by the end of the year and he's there, it's enough?"

"The time limit is December thirty-first. That's when you have to be married and the marriage has to be witnessed by the previous king."

"Then the ceremony we're having on the twenty-fourth should be fine as long as Father shows up." Charlie bit back a groan. His stepmother really must've hated him and his sister.

"Then we'd better ensure your father will arrive on time."

"Correct." He'd contact his father in a moment. "I should be enjoying my honeymoon, as it is, but I'm doing this."

"You're the king, sweetheart. You have duties." Spencer chuckled. "Abdicate or let Lender do it if the job is too hard."

"Over my dead body." Charlie gritted his teeth. Spencer's words rang all too true, despite annoying him. "Thank you, Spencer. Keep your ears and eyes open in case anything else happens. I'll call Father."

"Understood. I will." Spencer hung up.

Charlie groaned again. He didn't give a whit about what or who his father was doing in the States, but he did wish his father could tear himself away long enough to be a witness. Then again, this hiccup served Charlie right for rushing the wedding. He dialed his father's number and waited.

After four rings, his father answered. "Charlie, what's wrong?"

"Why do you think something is wrong? I can contact you to see how you're doing. How is your diplomatic mission going?" Charlie asked. "I hear things are progressing."

"They are. Carrie and I are having a lovely time," the former king said. "I mean…"

"Father, you can do as you please. You're an adult and single." He wandered around the bedroom. "But I do need you to come home soon."

"Did you decide to marry that young man? Nathan, is it?" his father asked. "He seems quite nice, from what I've seen. Pictures of him with you are all over the media here in the States. They're calling him the next prince of Lysianna."

"I don't know if he wants to be referred to as a prince, but I have married him and he is a wonderful man." He glanced over at River, who had sprawled on the bed.

"Wonderful. I can't wait to meet him," his father said. "Now what's the problem?"

"You will be here for Christmas, yes?"

"Unless something changes, yes. Why? If you've married him, then you're fine. That fulfills the decree," his father said. "I never liked that ridiculous decree."

"I'm glad to hear that, but you need to witness the wedding. I didn't know you needed to until we'd done it," Charlie said. "So my grand plan to marry him and get it over with so we can focus on enjoying Christmas, plus move on with our life, has sort of blown up."

"Go figure. Your stepmother, Elsie, could be a pain in my ass with her social climbing. I'm going to guess she thought you'd never get married," his father said.

"I'll be sure to arrive by the twenty-second, but I can come earlier. Did Lender pitch a fit?"

"A huge one. I haven't seen the latest installment, but Spencer has. Dad, I married Nathan because I love him. I want to be with him." Saying those words out loud felt so good.

"Did you want to marry him before you knew about the decree?"

"I didn't know him yet."

"Fair enough. If the decree were lifted without my being there, would you still love him?"

"Yes." Without question.

"Good. May I bring Carrie with me?"

"Sure." He paused. "Is she like Elsie?"

"Not a bit."

"Then fine." He wanted his father to be happy. "Tell me you'll be here. I know you said it before, but I'm worried. Oh, and will you stop calling it a diplomatic mission if it's not?"

"We'll get a flight out tomorrow," his father said. "And I'll call it what it is—a pleasure trip."

"Thanks. I'll see you when you arrive, and be safe."

"Of course. Enjoy your first night married."

Shit. He'd forgotten about Nathan. "I will. Night, Father."

"Night, kid."

He hung up with his father. Only his dad and mom called him kid. His stepmother never used that name. She hadn't been permitted. He tossed the phone onto the chair and turned his attention to Nathan. "I'm available. Sorry." He snorted. Instead of Nathan being naked, ready and waiting, he'd fallen asleep. Charlie couldn't blame him—they'd both had a long day.

Charlie crawled between the sheets with Nathan and held him close. Some might not call their wedding day ideal, but it was perfect for him. He had Nathan's love and now him as his husband. Once he adopted River, their life would be complete. He'd do his duty as king, but he didn't need the crown if he had his family.

* * * *

Nathan surfaced from sleep and moaned. He'd had the best dream. He and Charlie were married, but it had to be a dream. Guys like him, guys from Cleveland who worked as teachers, didn't marry kings. They didn't tread anywhere close to royalty.

He opened his eyes. Instead of Charlie next to him, the sheet moved. Charlie pulled the bedding down and grinned from his position by Nathan's hip.

"You're awake." Charlie tugged Nathan's shorts down his legs. "Before you ask—everything is fine. Mrs. Major has River, the door is closed and she won't interrupt us. My phone is on silent and we're allowed to do this, husband."

He sagged onto the mattress. Charlie had managed to assuage his fears in one fell swoop.

"And now, I'm going to show you how much I love you." Charlie settled between Nathan's legs. He stroked Nathan's dick and leaned over. "Like this."

Nathan flattened his hands on the bedding and enjoyed the show as Charlie kissed Nathan's inner thigh. At the same time, he stroked Nathan's cock. The caressing sent tingles through Nathan's system and fried his brain. Excitement overwhelmed him. The scent of Charlie lingered on his sheets and he loved the way Charlie touched him—so serene, but with passion and need. He felt Charlie in his soul.

He'd found a beautiful man in Charlie—one he never wanted to lose.

Charlie fondled Nathan's balls, drawing a sigh from deep within him. Electricity shot through him. He wriggled his hips, needing more from Charlie without saying a word. He rocked into Charlie's touch.

"Need me?" Charlie murmured and continued to pump his hand while he drew circles on Nathan's inner thigh with the tip of his tongue.

"Yes." He palmed Charlie's head. "Want you."

Charlie plunged his mouth down onto Nathan's shaft. Within seconds, he built into a steady rhythm. He flattened his tongue along the underside of Nathan's cock, then nibbled the blunt head. Before Nathan could react to the sizzles in his body, Charlie swallowed him deep.

Nathan couldn't think straight. So good. A simple blow job shouldn't make his synapses misfire—except Charlie knew how to make him fly. He groaned and pushed on Charlie's head.

Charlie increased his pace and caressed Nathan's asshole.

The move sent another tingle through Nathan. He bucked on the mattress and electricity spiraled in his body. He couldn't breathe. His muscles twitched and he dug his heels into the bedding. If Charlie did too much more, he'd blow.

Charlie hummed round him. At the same time, he toyed with Nathan's asshole.

"Oh God." Nathan bucked on the mattress. He gritted his teeth and jammed his cock into Charlie's mouth. His restraint was held by the thinnest thread. If Charlie hummed again, he'd go right over the edge.

Charlie groaned, then buried his nose in Nathan's curls.

Nathan let go of Charlie's head and grasped the sheets. He pistoned between Charlie's lips as the orgasm swept through him. He cried out, not caring if anyone heard him.

Instead of withdrawing, Charlie swallowed him deep again. He cleaned Nathan and rubbed his inner thighs.

Nathan sagged onto the sheets, fully spent. His mind was mush. How did Charlie do this to him?

Charlie sat back on his heels and grinned. "Love it?"

"I did," he managed. He panted. Charlie had worn him out and he'd just woken up.

Charlie collapsed beside him on the bed. "Good. I like making you happy."

"You do." Nathan tangled up with him. "I'm sorry I didn't stay awake last night. I couldn't keep my eyes open."

"You were tired. It's expected that you would be after yesterday." Charlie shrugged. "I didn't mind."

He relaxed. "What does today hold?" He was ready to embrace his new role, even if the thought of it sort of scared him, too. He'd married the king!

"Well…" Charlie tangled his legs with Nathan's and exhaled. "Today, we meet with the children of the kingdom while they decorate the courtyard evergreen trees with homemade ornaments. We'll meet with the assembly to officially present you to ensure they see you and know who you are. Plus, I need to meet with Spencer concerning my father's arrival."

"Is that all? There isn't much to do." He grinned. "When does your father get in?"

"As soon as possible, I hope," Charlie said. "Him getting here is a pressing issue."

"Oh. What's the issue? He doesn't need to meet me. He can come in when he's available." He wasn't that exciting.

"Actually, it's for you, but not entirely." Charlie tensed. "Part of what Spencer called about and interrupted us last night involved the wedding."

"What?" He laced his fingers with Charlie's to hide the tension. "What went wrong?"

"According to the decree, the former king needed to witness our marriage." Charlie sighed and kissed Nathan's knuckles. "We're legally married, but for our marriage to fulfill the decree, my father has to be here and see us exchange vows."

"So...whose idea was that?"

"My stepmother, who got the decree rushed into being and added to the protocols." Charlie exhaled and closed his eyes a moment. "When I'm finally installed as the king and have no restraints, that decree is getting dissolved."

"Probably good."

"So we have to drag the minister out to marry us again."

"What about the twenty-fourth? Is that too late?"

"Not entirely."

"Then he doesn't have to rush." He didn't see any reason to make the former king hurry or why there had to be so many weddings. One should've been enough. "Seems wasteful to do this over and over, too."

"In a way it is, but in a lot of ways, it's expected." Charlie cuddled up to him. "When my parents got married, they had four weddings. Four! Why? Because the first time, they ran off and made it legal. The second time was for my grandparents to witness it, along with my other set of grandparents. I don't know why they had to watch it that way, but they did."

"Okay…" That made two.

"Then they had to have a wedding in her country, then the official huge wedding in front of the kingdom." Charlie laughed. "They hated it because it was done so many times, but the whole thing wasn't unexpected since everyone had to witness it."

"Will we have to go through that four times? I would, but I heard the arguments about the cost." He'd never forget the complaining, and truth be told, he agreed. Once was enough, even if he'd marry Charlie a thousand times over.

"As long as father makes it here by the twenty-fourth, we'll be fine." Charlie kissed him. "The other thing is Lender. He's upset that it's even possible we could be married, so I'm keeping River in the palace. He's not going to the ornament hanging or anything. Not until Father is our witness. I won't risk him getting hurt."

He appreciated Charlie's consideration. If Nathan thought life was going to be easy instead of scary, he had another think coming. Until the threats were gone, he'd have to keep checking over his shoulder.

"You have to know this won't be the last time something shitty will happen. I never know when someone will get the idea to get violent, but that's why we have protection and minimize risks," Charlie said. "And we vet people."

"True." He sighed as the heaviness of the moment weighed on him.

"Come with me to the shower. We'll get cleaned up and refreshed." Charlie disengaged from him and sat up. "Plus we can enjoy each other in there."

"Lead the way." Nathan left the bed and padded naked into the adjacent bathroom. He couldn't wait to be with Charlie in every way possible.

Chapter Thirteen

Nathan raked his fingers through his hair and watched his lover move. Charlie was like poetry in motion, so smooth and graceful. Just a look from him sent shivers through Nathan's body.

Charlie turned on the water and stripped out of his shorts. He stood nude before Nathan. "I hope you like what you see. I can't change it."

"Who said you should?" He trailed his fingers over Charlie's abs. He spotted the ink on Charlie's hip and gasped. "You have a tattoo." He'd never noticed it before. "Since when?"

"Since I was nineteen." Charlie blushed, then dragged Nathan into the stall. "I had this misguided notion I needed a crown at all times, so I got one inked onto my body. But when the time came to get the actual tattoo, I realized I didn't want everyone to see it or for it to show up in photos, so I had it hidden. Even my father doesn't know about it."

"I take it he'd be upset?" He stepped into the shower. The water sluiced over him, stinging and hot, but relaxing. "I'm too chicken to get a tattoo."

"It takes commitment." Charlie lathered the washcloth. "You have your own version — you're a dad. That's a badge of honor."

"Remember that when he's throwing up on you." He groaned as Charlie washed his body. "That feels good."

"Kid barf?" Charlie laughed. "No, I knew what you meant. There's something about a good, hot shower that fixes a lot. It revives you."

"It does." The bubbles slid down his chest. "It unknots the muscles."

Charlie grinded on Nathan's hip. "Plus, the slipperiness of the soap helps lube everything." He reached around Nathan and caressed his cock. He situated his own dick between Nathan's ass cheeks. The soap did add lubrication to the action.

Heat flowed in Nathan's veins. "Charlie." He shuddered. "Oh God."

"Yeah?" Charlie stroked faster and rocked against Nathan's butt. "Feels good."

He panted and braced himself on the wall with his hands. "Charlie." His thoughts scrambled again.

"I love it." Charlie nipped Nathan's shoulder. "You fit me so well. You're made for me."

Nathan moved his hips in time with Charlie's sliding He needed this. He'd just come, but already the orgasm was building. The tiles warmed under his palms and the hot water slid down his back, but the hottest thing was the man holding him. Droplets stuck to his eyelashes and made it hard to see, but he didn't care.

"Want me?" Charlie asked. "Husband?"

He'd never get tired of hearing that. "Yes, husband. Fuck me." He bucked into Charlie. He had no idea what Charlie was using, but something slid down the crack of his ass. He widened his stance, expecting Charlie to penetrate him.

"Hold on." Charlie toyed with Nathan's puckered skin. "Relax. Gotta prep you." He pushed his finger in and out of Nathan.

He did the best he could, but there wasn't much relaxing around Charlie. The excitement was almost too much. He undulated against Charlie. "Do it." He couldn't wait any longer. He needed Charlie inside him. Besides, it wouldn't take long for him to come. Not now.

Charlie let go of Nathan's dick and withdrew his finger from his ass. He grasped Nathan's hips and pushed against him, penetrating him inch by inch, until he was fully within him.

He groaned at the burn from being stretched, and the fullness. The momentary pain shifted to pleasure in seconds. He met Charlie thrust for thrust. The sound of the water roared in his ears and the droplets stung his body, but Charlie overwhelmed his senses.

"Fuck." Charlie ratcheted up the pace. His fingers bit into Nathan's skin. He groaned. "Need you."

He couldn't argue, but he also couldn't take much more. His knees quaked. He splayed one hand on the tiles and wrapped his other hand around his cock. "Charlie."

"God, yes. Let go." Charlie increased his tempo again.

His restraint cracked. The combination of his hand on his dick, Charlie in his ass and the thrill of the moment were his undoing. His movements turned feral as he came again. From head to toe, his body seemed to float. He wasn't the same man as before. He'd changed and become better because of Charlie. He'd found his dual purpose—being with Charlie and being a dad. Cum shot onto the wall and he closed his eyes.

"Fuck." Charlie rammed into him, pinning him to the tiles.

Nathan didn't mind the pressure. The chilly wall quelled some of his fever.

"Nathan." Charlie cried out and filled him to the hilt. His cock throbbed within Nathan. He slumped against him and groaned.

Nathan listened to the cadence of the water flowing and basked in the perfection of the moment. He and Charlie were one.

Charlie held tight to him. "I knew this would be good, but you're better than good. You're the best."

"Sexy is stronger when you're with your husband." He fought to catch his breath.

"Yes." Charlie sighed and pulled out. "We should really shower now. I have no idea when I'm due for the first event."

"Then let me wash you." Nathan scrubbed his lover clean, making sure he fondled and caressed every bit of him.

"God." Charlie quickly returned the favor. "You'll get me hard again with the way you touch me."

"Maybe that was the point." Nathan rinsed and waited for Charlie to finish before he left the stall. "I want you to find me irresistible."

"I do." Charlie turned the water off and dried himself, then Nathan. "I'm going to have Spencer bring me some clothes. Need anything?"

"No." He wrapped the towel around his waist. "I have a couple questions, though." No time like the present to ask the things he'd logged in his mind.

"Shoot." Charlie grabbed the second towel and wandered out to the bedroom. While covered with the towel, he retrieved his phone. "What's up?"

"Does Spencer help with your outfits? I know this sounds incredibly selfish or maybe even materialistic, but should I have a plan for my clothes? Should I be putting more thought into what I'm wearing? Are there protocols?" He'd asked so much, but the queries spilled out. "Sorry."

"Don't be sorry." Charlie finished whatever he was doing on his phone. "I've thrown you into a huge situation with almost no guidance."

"Sort of." He selected a pair of boxer shorts from the dresser. "I don't want to show up in the wrong clothes—something too formal for a casual event or something too casual for a formal one."

Charlie donned the underwear he'd worn the night before and sat on the bed. "First, you'll have access to Spencer for your clothing choices because you'll be living with me in the royal suite and he's my advisor. So once you're installed in my quarters, you'll have help. Until then, just ask. I'll help you and so will Spencer. Second, this is why you were fitted for those suits. Your own clothes are fine, but this will help you be prepared. Third, you can select your attire ahead of time if you choose, but ask if you're worried. That's fine. As for the protocols, there really aren't any, but you're expected to dress well because you're with the king. I've been told too much informality telegraphs poor planning and presentation. I don't know that I completely buy into that, but it's possible to be too informal."

"Okay." That helped, but not too much.

"Wear a nice sweater with a button-down underneath. Pair them with dark jeans or slacks and casual dress shoes. Black socks if you have them, and a nice watch, too," Charlie said. "We'll be running around, so no suits."

"I've never been much of a fashion plate." He withdrew a sweater and dark blue button-down from the closet. "Will this work?"

"Perfect." Charlie toyed with the sleeve of the sweater. "I have one in the same general color scheme. I'll find it and try not to wear it at the same time so we don't look strange and match."

"Smart." He picked out a pair of dark blue jeans. "I dressed up for my graduation and the few job opportunities I landed, but I never thought I looked right."

"I'm sure you looked wonderful." Charlie stood. "Spencer is here."

"Does he mind you being in your underwear?" Nathan asked. It seemed rather strange to be addressing someone in his boxers.

"He's seen worse." Charlie opened the door to Spencer. "Hi."

"Hi." Spencer strode into the room and grinned at Nathan. "Hi. Did you have a good night?"

"It was." Nathan dressed while Charlie conferred with Spencer. He adjusted the button-down beneath the sweater, then fastened his belt. He didn't have a fancy watch. All he possessed was his simple leather-banded version.

Spencer turned to Nathan. "I hear you need style advice."

"It couldn't hurt." Nathan stepped back. "I tried."

"You've done well. You look good and we'll set you up with some accessories this week to add to the overall effect." Spencer walked around him. "Yes, you'll do."

"Oh, thanks." He watched Charlie dress.

"Give me an hour and we'll go to the children's event," Charlie said. "I'll have Spencer retrieve you. Zara and Luke are going to be there as well."

"Okay." He wanted to see River, so the time worked for him.

"You look great," Charlie said. "I'm sorry this has been so messed up, but once we get this sorted out, we'll have a real honeymoon. How about after Christmas?" He kissed Nathan. "Somewhere warm?"

Nathan shrugged. "This whole situation is like one gigantic dream. It's fine if we stay here for now."

"It'll get better. I love you." Charlie kissed him a second time, then left Nathan alone in the bedroom.

Spencer lingered a second. "You're doing well and we're all here to help you."

"Thanks." Nathan sighed as Spencer vacated the room, too. He'd spent a lot of time away from River. Yes, he and Charlie deserved some time together, but that didn't make him feel any less guilty for not seeing River.

He ventured out of the bedroom. He might be married to the king, but it was time to step back into reality.

* * * *

Charlie finished the briefing before heading out to his office. He had too much to do today. According to Spencer's information, King Martin should've landed by now and been on his way to the castle. He worried his father wouldn't arrive on time or something would go wrong. The pressure on everyone to make the second wedding ceremony come off perfectly was more than it should've been.

"Where are they?" Charlie strode along the corridor. "I haven't heard a thing from Father." He needed updates.

"The plane landed, but there are issues with the car." Spencer stopped in the middle of the hall. "Oh shit."

Charlie halted as well. "What?" His blood chilled. "Talk to me."

Spencer paled. "There was an accident." He gulped. "The car containing your father and his paramour exploded when rammed by another vehicle on the tarmac. It's believed the other vehicle carried the explosive device. As of now, there is no word on the casualties and no suspects."

His heart dropped. He had to get to Zara. The world seemed to blur around him and his knees weakened. He leaned against the wall, then righted himself. For all he knew, his father wasn't dead. He could be safe, right? *Could've survived.* Until he knew for sure, he needed to keep a cool head. The kingdom needed him to be controlled.

"What do we do?" Spencer wobbled. "I'm trying to get updates."

"We go to Zara and tell her." He stood straight and marched down the corridor. This was no time to fall apart.

Every cell in his body was on high alert. Who would try to harm King Martin? Someone who wished to stop the royal wedding, for one. Was it Lender? "Where is the man who thinks he'll be the king?"

"Lender? Unaccounted for." Spencer rushed to keep up with him. "The royal police have been dispatched to his home as well as the residence of your former stepmother."

"Very well." He rushed to Zara's quarters and knocked. "Zara? I need to speak with you. Now."

"Just a moment." She opened the door. Alistair wriggled in her arms. A food stain marred her T-shirt and her hair had been captured in a sloppy ponytail. "What's wrong?"

"Father has been potentially injured." He rushed into the suite. "There are reports of an explosion."

Luke wandered into the room with a teething cookie. He handed the cookie to Alistair. "Hi, Charlie."

She gave Luke the baby. "Take him. I need to speak with Charlie."

"Sure." Luke grabbed Alistair and left the room.

Zara scrubbed her face with the back of her hand. "There was an accident?"

"Yes. I don't have the full extent of the damage," Charlie said. "I'm sorry."

"It's not as bad as you think." She looked him in the eye. "They weren't on that flight or in that car."

"What?" He had to sit down. "Zara?" Nothing made sense.

"Daddy confided to me that he thought something would happen if they took that flight, so they arrived at four this morning and drove from another airport. He refused to tell me which one, but he's here in the castle."

His stomach roiled. At least his father was safe, but someone could've let him know the truth before now. "You didn't think I should know? Why?"

"You were on your honeymoon of sorts and it wasn't that pressing. We thought it was a silly premonition and wouldn't amount to anything…then it did." She sat across from him. "You needed to take time with your husband. I know it's not good for us to have kept this from you, but I had this under control and you had a good night with Nathan."

He wanted to be angry, but his gratefulness for her planning won out. "Tell me the story."

"I guess Daddy got a bad feeling when they were on the way to the airport. He didn't give me all the details, but he thought someone was following him, so they took the next available flight and drove here after they landed. The official records weren't updated, so it appeared they arrived just a bit ago."

He sighed. "Okay." He was starting to sound like Nathan. "Do you know where they are?" Part of him cursed his need for a private life and not being on watch, but the rest of him chided himself for not giving himself a break. "I need to find them. I need to see for myself that they're not harmed." The crisis was the biggest thing he'd ever dealt with and he was determined not to screw up. His family needed him to be strong.

Chapter Fourteen

Charlie raked his fingers through his hair and tried to come up with all the possibilities for what might have happened to his father. Sure, he wanted King Martin to witness the wedding, but mostly, he wanted his father to be all right.

Luke, carrying Alistair, returned to the room and stood next to Zara. "We have guests." He stepped aside. King Martin and his girlfriend ventured into the space.

Zara blushed. "Sorry, Charlie. I didn't want their location to leak. The car was bombed and everyone worried it'd get worse."

"And no one thought to slip me a note?" Charlie stood and embraced his father. "I need to get Spencer to figure out what happened."

"I can tell you," King Martin said. "I read the article in the papers where Lender bragged that the royal wedding wasn't legitimate and he deserved the crown. Then when we were at the airport, there was a man following us. It could've been innocent, but you know that feeling—the odd one that makes you pause. I had it and decided to just leave right then. I'm glad I did. Then, knowing the people your stepmother consorted with, I assumed something was in the works and it was better to get the hell out of there."

"So you switched flights?" Charlie asked. "And cars?"

"And kept a low profile." King Martin moved aside. "This is Carrie Lillard. I met her on the cruise ship. She and I were going to the same party at the art museum. She introduced me to the movers and shakers in the States."

"Hi." He smiled, but kept his emotions guarded for the moment. Plenty of people had tried to get in good with the royal family—like his stepmother—and this woman might be perfectly fine, but he needed to be sure. "It's nice to meet you."

"Likewise." She stayed beside King Martin and didn't say much, which Charlie appreciated.

"As long as you're okay, I'm good." Charlie sighed. "I want you to meet Nathan." He'd also like his heartrate to return to a normal level.

"Will he be at the decorating event?" King Martin asked.

"Yes, but not with his little boy." Charlie texted Nathan, then Spencer. They needed to add extra layers of protection to the event. He wanted no chance for Lender to slip in.

"He's got a son?" Carrie asked. "I have two grandchildren—a boy and a girl."

"Nice." He shoved his phone into his pocket. "Since this isn't the huge thing I thought it was, I can get back to handling today's events." He paused. "I'm also having the minister brought up as soon as possible. I want the crown secured and for the ball to be a celebration."

"Smart." King Martin stepped into the hallway with him. "Son, may I have a moment with you?"

"Sure." He had all the time in the word. "I'm glad you're okay."

"I am. Now, I want to tell you about Carrie. She's a widow and very sweet. She's two years younger than me and I had my advisors fully vet her, like I should've done with your stepmother. She's a good person and doesn't need our money. She's got her husband's wealth, which has been nice because we've kept things equal and even."

"Dad, if you're happy, then that's what matters." He folded his arms. "And you're here in one piece, so that's the biggest thing. Yes, I'm being selfish. I don't want the crown to slip into Lender's hands, so I know I sound terrible and guarded."

"It's understandable." King Martin laughed. "If I'd had that decree in place when I married your mother, she would've left me high and dry. It's a pain, all these weddings. But Nathan seems to be worth it. May I meet him?

"Yes." His phone buzzed and he checked the notification. Nathan and Spencer were on the way to the office, and so was the minister. "They're on the way."

"Carrie will be fine with your sister. Let's go, but let me tell them where I'm going." King Martin left for a moment, then returned and closed the door. "Ready."

Charlie put his phone away. He had no idea how Lender or anyone else knew which car to bomb and it bothered him. *Damn it.* He should've been on top of such details. He fell into step with his father. "How'd you know you were ready to move on with Carrie?"

"It happened quite innocently. She kept showing up at the same places and I finally had Krieger check her out. Everything he found was perfectly normal. Then we started talking and I kept my being a royal secret. I wanted her to like me without knowing I was a king."

"I had the same idea with Nathan, but when he found out, he was livid that I'd lied by omission. Boy, he was upset." He stepped into his office. "Was she?"

"Initially, yes. She thought I'd been underhanded — which I was — and she was right to be angry. Then I confessed everything to her and we discussed the mistakes I'd made with your stepmother. Namely, I admitted the biggest blunder was not involving you kids, but I learned my lesson. If I knew then what I learned later, that she was going to be so cruel to you kids, I'd have steered away."

He would've liked for his father not to have married Elsie, too.

"But it worked out." King Martin sat on the edge of Charlie's desk. "Please don't fall into the same traps I did and forget your family or ignore their needs because you think you're saving the country. They need you the most."

"Once I get through this, I'll be fine. Speaking of getting through, I don't know what title to give Nathan so he's protected. I don't know what to do for River, his son, either." He paced the length of the office. "I need to adopt him — no, I want to. He needs both parents, but there's his surrogate to consider. When she finds out Nathan's married to me, she might decide she wants custody or to make waves."

"You'll have to handle that when it happens—if it happens," King Martin said.

Spencer rushed into the room. "Good. You're both here." He bowed to Charlie, then to Martin. "So, the first thing is, I'm glad you're here and safe. I had the wording drawn up that you'd perished, but hesitated to put the statement out. I'm glad I waited."

"I'm very much alive," King Martin said. "Thanks for your patience."

"You're welcome. Now, the second thing is from the police. The bomb squad and the royal police have the cars in their possession and video footage from the time of the explosion. The person in the bombed car, the crashed one, is deceased. He was identified as Lender's footman. Lender wasn't on the scene and has been spotted in a royal café."

"Of course." Charlie groaned and resumed pacing the length of the office. "Is he loose?"

"He is," Spencer said. "The third thing concerns Lender. He can't be arrested as of yet because the footman left a suicide note—which is in dispute— declaring he'd done this to ensure Lender got the crown. Lender claims no knowledge of the letter or intent."

"I'm sure he doesn't," King Martin said.

"The fourth thing is this." Spencer produced a box. "These are wedding rings, all in size eleven. It turns out you and Nathan are the same size, and he's on his way here, so you might want to select the rings before he arrives."

Charlie gazed at the jewelry. He should take his time, but he didn't have much. Every moment he thought he'd secured the crown, something went sideways. The faster he sorted this out and made the marriage binding, the better.

He looked at the rings again. Did they really need fancy rings to show their love? *No.* He selected two simple gold bands. "These," Charlie said.

"Good choice," King Martin said. "Smart."

"Thanks." *Now, where are they?* "I want the full report from the accident and a watch on Lender. Also, are there any other caveats to the decree? Like Lender has to watch? Or we have to stand on our heads? Huh? Anyone?"

"The king has to witness the wedding this time and the minister has to preside over it." Spencer opened the door. "Here's the groom and minister."

Nathan and Father Kaplan entered the office. "We're doing this again?" Father Kaplan asked. "Is everyone who needs to be here present?"

Nathan nodded. "I am."

"I am," King Martin said. "Before we do anything else, Nathan, I'm King Martin, Charlie's father. I've heard a lot about you and I'm honored you've decided to join our family." He held out his hand.

Nathan glanced over at Charlie, then shook hands with the king. "It's an honor to meet you. I'm still learning the protocols and stuff, but I'm glad we've finally been introduced."

"Now, Spencer, you'll be the witness, correct?" King Martin asked. "Let's get this going."

"I am, and I'm recording everything on my phone, too." Spencer held up the device. "I have King Charles, King Martin, Father Kaplan and Nathan Pratt, plus me, Lord Spencer, present on this twelfth day of December to witness the marriage of Nathan Pratt to King Charles."

Charlie exhaled and the pressure released within him. *Thank God.* Time to move forward and marry his husband again so he could keep the crown where it belonged and Nathan in his arms.

"Ready?" Father Kaplan nodded. "We gather here today to celebrate the union of our king, King Charles, and Nathan Pratt in holy matrimony. Love is the glue to bind us together. It can destroy and cause pain, but love can also be salvation and comfort. Today, we champion the union of these two men and their love."

Charlie gazed at Nathan. He'd marry Nathan a thousand times without the threat of losing the crown hanging over his head. He held Nathan's hands and basked in the passion between them.

"Now, Nathan Pratt, do you take this man, our king, as your husband? Will you love, trust and honor him all the days of your life and devote yourself to growing the union?" Father Kaplan asked. "If so, say 'I do'."

Charlie's heart hammered. He and Nathan were already married, but he still anticipated Nathan's answer.

"I do," Nathan said. "Always."

Thank God.

"Our king, do you take this man, Nathan Pratt, as your husband? Will you trust love and honor him all the days of your life and devote yourself to growing the union?" Father Kaplan asked. "If so, say 'I do'."

"I do." Charlie didn't need any prompting on this one.

"May I have the rings?" Father Kaplan asked.

King Martin offered up the jewelry. Nathan let go of Charlie's hands long enough to switch the ruby ring into his right hand.

"Nathan?" Father Kaplan handed him one of the rings. "You may speak the words on your heart."

Charlie braced himself. He wasn't sure what Nathan might say.

"Charlie, the day I saw you in the solarium, something told me to go to you. I wanted to make you happy. I don't know if I'll always be able to take away your sadness, but I'll endeavor to make your life better. I will love you more each day because you're the part of my family, the one River and I didn't know we needed but can't live without. We're happy to share our lives with you. To prove that, I give you this ring." He held up the jewelry, then slipped it onto Charlie's finger.

Tears blurred in Charlie's eyes. He hadn't planned to get weepy, but Nathan's words got to him. Charlie flexed his hand. The ring weighed more than he thought, but it was the best reminder that he wasn't alone. He blinked back tears. "I love you, Nathan."

Nathan smiled. "Love you, too."

"Our king, you may speak the words on your heart," Father Kaplan said.

Charlie gulped to get a hold of himself. "Nathan, I never thought I could love someone in the way I do you. You make me smile when I'm down, laugh when I'm upset and ground me. I can't imagine my life without you and River. I'll take the late nights, the messy diapers, the struggles of being a parent, because I have you. You're the partner I never knew I needed and you're exactly the one I want, too." He fumbled with the ring, then slipped it onto Nathan's finger. "Which is why I give you this ring to symbolize our union."

"Love you," Nathan murmured. His eyes shimmered and he smiled. The love and warmth in his smile thrilled Charlie.

"I love you, too." Charlie held Nathan's hands again.

"Now, by the power vested in me and by the witness of King Martin, I now pronounce you husband and husband. You may kiss your husband."

Charlie didn't wait for Father Kaplan to finish his statement. He needed this kiss more than his next breath. He embraced Nathan and kissed him. His world righted and life seemed normal again. He'd done it. He'd married Nathan again, with his father as the witness. Spencer had recorded the event for posterity. No one could argue this hadn't happened. Let Lender have a shit fit. He had no standing.

Charlie had the crown and now also the man of his heart.

Chapter Fifteen

Nathan relaxed as he shook hands with people at the children's ornament event. He hadn't quite caught his breath from the wedding, just an hour before. He couldn't believe he'd met the former king, had married Charlie again and was an official royal. He couldn't help but look at his left hand and the gold ring. He'd become part of the family, and they'd discussed his title. He didn't need a title.

The line of people ended and Nathan took his position on the small stage with Charlie. King Martin and Carrie were there as well as Princess Charlie and Prince Luke.

Carrie half-smiled. "Feels strange being here. I'm not royalty. I don't want to be."

"It's not so bad." What did he know? He'd only been part of the family for a few weeks.

"I see how you look at Charlie and it's sweet. You can tell how much you love each other," she said. "Everyone should have love like that."

"I hope you find love that way, too." He appreciated her honesty, but also her guts for sticking it out with the king. She could've taken one look at the pandemonium around them and left. A bombing, fake cars, subterfuge…it was a lot to handle.

Charlie held up his hand. "Friends, citizens of Lysianna. Welcome to the annual decorating festivities here at the castle. We're excited to have this event. It's one of my favorite times of the year because the grounds look so festive. I'm excited to see what the children of Lysianna have come up with this year. Now, in addition to Princess Zara and Prince Luke, King Martin has graced with his presence today and has brought along his girlfriend, Carrie Lillard. I hope you will welcome her as warmly as you have embraced me. We also have someone quite important to me here today. My fiancé, Nathan Pratt, has joined me. He is incredibly special and I'm sure you'll come to love him as much as I do."

The crowd erupted in cheers, and Nathan stuck close to Charlie. He'd never been good with throngs of people and the noise bothered him a bit, but this was part of life with Charlie, so he had no choice but to go along. He nodded and waved a bit.

"Should I be doing something besides waving?" he murmured.

"You're fine," King Martin said. "Just be yourself."

Charlie squeezed Nathan's hand. "On behalf of the royal family, we welcome the children of Lysianna to decorate the trees of the courtyard for everyone in the kingdom to enjoy."

The children rushed to the trees and Charlie stepped away from the microphone. He exhaled and nodded. "Now, we wait for the kids to finish. We'll wander around the trees after a bit, but for now, we admire from up here."

"The kids love decorating," Zara said. "I'm going to pitch in and help."

"I'll come with." Luke followed her into the crowd. Their security team followed behind to keep them safe.

King Martin left the dais to help children with decorations on the closest tree.

"What do we do? I feel like a sitting duck up here." Nathan fidgeted. "I know it looks bad that I'm hesitant, but it's so exposed."

"Then we go into the crowd." Charlie held his hand and accompanied Nathan into the courtyard. The laughter of children rang out and people stopped to shake hands with Charlie.

Nathan smiled and shook hands with those who offered. Something bothered him. Sure, Charlie said they were safe and the security detail followed them through the crowd, but he couldn't shake the uneasiness. Would this be his life from now on? Looking over his shoulder? He hoped not. He held tight to Charlie's arm. There were so many people. Lots of kids, too. He couldn't help his discomfort in the crowd. He spotted a man staring at them. He shouldn't be shocked, though. Weren't the people of Lysianna going to watch them? Besides that, he was an anomaly—a strange person in the group of royals.

Still, this creeped him out.

Charlie helped a little girl hang a wreath on the closest tree. Nathan forced a smile. Being among the loyal subjects felt right, but wrong at the same time. Lender could be anywhere.

The staring man inched closer and Nathan clutched Charlie's forearm. "Charlie?" He had to be cool and not attract attention while still letting Charlie know. "Charlie?"

"It'll be fine." Charlie slid his gaze over Nathan. "Nathan? You're going to rip my arm off. Don't be scared. The people just want to look at you."

"It's not that, Charlie. Something isn't right." He shivered. "I'm trying to keep a brave face, but I don't trust...*him*." He spotted someone out of the corner of his eye and his blood chilled. Was it truly Lender? Or a figment of his imagination?

"What do you see?" Charlie asked.

"I could swear Lender is here." Nathan squeezed Charlie's hand. "It might not be him, but I can't shake this feeling."

Charlie gestured to the security team. One of the members, a blond man, strode forward as Charlie moved away from the group of children.

"Where is Lender?" Charlie asked. "Please? I need to know."

"At his home, last we knew. I'll get precise information." The blond man turned away from them. "I need a direct location on the target."

"Charlie? Where is your sister?" Nathan asked.

"Over there." Charlie tensed. "Is the guy in the blue jacket with the red patch the one you're concerned about?"

"Yes." He couldn't look. "He's been hovering."

"Because it's Lender," Charlie snapped. He stepped between Nathan and Lender.

Before Charlie could speak, Nathan heard something crack and his ribs ached. He crumpled forward and gripped his abdomen. Everything ached. He hadn't eaten today and this wasn't his stomach roiling. This was worse. He looked at Charlie, but whatever his husband said, Nathan couldn't make it out. "Charlie?"

"Oh my God." A woman yanked her child back. "He's bleeding."

Nathan wobbled. "Help?" His hands were covered in red. Blood?

King Martin caught Nathan before he tumbled to the ground. "Jesus. He's been shot. Security!"

Charlie whipped around and seemed to move in slow motion. "Fuck."

Nathan wanted to tell Charlie not to use such coarse language, but the words weren't there. He felt himself being lifted onto something, but it was more like an out of body experience. No matter what he tried, he couldn't get anyone's attention or make noise. His chest hurt and he couldn't forget the blood on his hands.

His blood?

Oh shit.

Charlie's life seemed to flash before his eyes as he watched the medics carry Nathan away. Nathan was bleeding. He'd been hurt. How was this possible? It was because Charlie had opted to spend time with the people down in the crowd. He knew better than to mingle at this stage of the festivities, but he'd allowed his duty to the people win out over his common sense.

"Now you can't be king." Lender shoved Charlie. "He's dead, so you don't have a husband."

Charlie glared at Lender. All his pent-up rage bubbled to the surface. This man had pushed him around for long enough. He had to behave with decorum, but that didn't mean he couldn't put Lender in his place.

"What are you going to do?" Lender snapped. "He's dead."

"You have no idea." He held up one hand. "If he is dead, then it's on you. Only someone who was involved would jump to such conclusions." He flicked his fingers. "Guards, put him in the dungeon until further notice. I want the attacker captured immediately."

"Yes, my king." The guard nabbed Lender.

Charlie ensured his sister, brother-in-law, father and Carrier were safely in the castle, then spoke with the guards before he left the scene. He needed to get to Nathan.

Please let him be okay.

Charlie rushed to the royal hospital and his heart lodged in his throat. He couldn't lose Nathan. Not now. Besides, River couldn't lose his father.

Charlie burst into the ER. "I need to see my husband."

"My king." The nurse bowed. "I will make sure you see him as soon as he's out of surgery."

"What happened?" *Surgery? Shit, shit, shit.* "Where is the doctor?"

King Martin rushed into the room, then steered Charlie into a private waiting room. "We need to act with dignity."

"I know." He paced the smaller room. "We've just started our relationship and River needs his dad. This isn't fair. Did I make the wrong decision by bringing them into the family? I put them at risk. Dad...I might have gotten him killed." It was a terrible thought, but possible.

"No one's said he's perished. Lender spoke out of turn and wanted to upset you—which he has." King

Martin grabbed Charlie by the shoulders. "You have to believe Nathan will pull through and the security team will apprehend the man who shot him. I know it's hard, but it's what you have to do."

"Did I make the wrong decision, though? I knew better than to go out into the crowd, but I thought this was a party, not a chance to risk Nathan's life." Charlie shook his head. "I knew better."

"You couldn't know Lender would be there. The last anyone was notified, he was still under surveillance at the café." King Martin slid his phone from his pocket. "Just a moment." He stood at the edge of the room and spoke in hushed tones.

Charlie debated his next move. He should be there for the people, but Nathan was one of the people, too. So was River.

"Sire?" A man stepped into the room. "King Charles?"

Charlie snapped out of his thoughts and focused on the man. "You're the doctor?"

"I am. Dr. Warren. It's a pleasure to meet you. Now, I've had the honor of taking care of your husband. As he's part of the royal family, I'm at liberty to give you updates." The doctor shoved his hands into his pockets. "First, the wound, a gunshot wound, was a through and through. He was quite lucky as the bullet missed all vital organs, so either the shooter was a lousy shot or extremely good as to not cause as much damage. Also because he's part of the royal family, he's been moved and he's gone."

Charlie wobbled on his feet. *Gone?* He had to have heard the doctor incorrectly. "I'm sorry. You said he's gone?"

"Yes, he's been moved to the royal medical suite in the castle. He'll still have round the clock care, but he'll be with the family instead of here at the hospital. He won't be mobile for a day or two, but as soon as he's feeling up to moving, he should be. I'm going to trust you'll take care of him?"

"Yes." Charlie hugged the doctor. "Thank you." Tears burned at the corners of his eyes. The pressure of holding on to the crown, the potential of losing Nathan and the excitement of the last few days had finally worn on him.

"You're welcome, my king." The doctor let go. "I'm going to check in on him this evening and tomorrow morning, but he'll be tired for the next few hours."

"Understandable." Charlie nodded and composed himself. "Then we'll head over to the royal suite. Thank you."

King Martin nodded. "Thank you, Dr. Warren. You're a credit to the crown." He nodded once, then ushered Charlie from the room. "We'll go right to the royal suites."

"Thanks, Father." He appreciated more than ever his father being there. "I'm sorry I've been so pushy. I've thought of nothing but myself."

"You're stressed." King Martin escorted Charlie through the castle. "When your mother died, I thought my life had ended. I didn't want to get out of bed or face the people. All I wanted to do was hide and considered ending my own life. I couldn't see living without Ria."

"You never told me that." He slowed his pace a bit. Getting his father to open up wasn't easy, and if the king wanted to talk, he'd listen.

"You don't remember how sick she was, but those headaches were unbearable sometimes. She'd stay in bed and I'd take you kids to the courtyard to play to give her peace, but it always pained me. I wanted to help her. Even when we found out about the tumor, I wanted to fix it. Now you understand my helplessness. I couldn't talk to you or your sister at the time because you were hurting, too. But it was you two who brought me out of my funk. I couldn't let you be raised by my parents or nannies. I know I wasn't the best father, but I tried, and if I could go back for a do-over, I would. Sometimes I wonder if I made your mother proud with the way I raised you."

"You did the best you could." He'd once hated his father for letting Mother leave without telling them goodbye. Once he'd learned the truth, the hatred disappeared. His father was right, though. Now he understood the pain of loss and could almost understand his father's behavior.

"You have the chance to do better than I did. You will adopt River and give him two fathers who love him. You'll make sure he grows up strong and is the best version of himself he can be." King Martin stopped outside of the royal quarters. "I had him and Mrs. Major brought over here to be with Nathan."

"Thank you." He hadn't even thought of that. "I feel so ill-equipped. Like I'm messing this up."

"There isn't exactly a rule book." King Martin hugged Charlie. "Just love him as much as you can and help him without hovering. He needs you to be strong."

"I will." He grasped the door handle, then dragged a breath into his lungs to steady himself before exhaling and entering the room.

Mrs. Major sat on the sofa with River against her chest. "Don't slam the door," she murmured. "I just got him to sleep. He's sleeping, too."

Charlie crept across the room to Nathan's bed. He drank in the details of Nathan's face, so ashen. His dark lashes contrasted with the paleness of his cheeks. The hospital gown covered the wound and Charlie debated moving the garment to look at the bandaging. Instead, he sat on the edge of the bed and placed his hand on Nathan's, trying not to jostle him too much.

Nathan opened his eyes and a weak smile curled at the corners of his mouth. "Hi."

"Hi. Don't talk." Charlie rubbed the top of Nathan's hand. "You're awake. I thought I lost you. Thought the world had come to an end. I can't do this without you beside me."

"You've got the crown," Nathan managed. "That's what matters."

The tears he'd been holding back since the moment he'd seen Nathan carted away finally overflowed. He couldn't hold back if he tried. "No." His voice cracked and he didn't care. "I know it seemed like I had the worst idea when I proposed we get married so I could keep the crown, but I was wrong. I knew all along I wanted to be with you. No one else ever treated me like a normal person. You've been special since the moment we met. I can't do this without you and the crown doesn't mean anything if you're not beside me. I love you and I always will."

Nathan's smile increased just a little. "I love you, too." He sighed. "What happened to Lender?"

"He's in the dungeon. We have one and he's there. I don't know about the other assailant." He should summon Spencer. "Things have happened so fast."

"Charlie?" King Martin gestured to Lord Spencer. "Your advisor is here. I'm going to check on the rest of the family."

"Thank you." Charlie kept hold of Nathan's hand and turned his attention to his advisor. "Spencer."

"Well...shit." Spencer sighed. "Sorry. I forgot myself for a moment."

"It's been one hell of a day," Nathan said.

He'd said a mouthful. Charlie rubbed his free hand on his lap. "What's the word, Spencer?"

Spencer held up his tablet. "First, I'm glad Sir Nathan is recovering. It's wonderful to see you, even if you are injured. At least you're alive."

"We're all thankful for that." Charlie winked at Nathan. He genuinely loved this man.

"Second, Lender is in the dungeon and swears he knew nothing about the plot to remove Sir Nathan. Unfortunately, his accomplice, Clayborne George, confessed to everything. He admitted to placing the bomb in the car meant for your father, as well as shooting Nathan, and he's got the handwritten notice from Lender directing him to do so. Lender's prints are on the document and it's very obvious it's his handwriting. Both are in the dungeon with no chance of getting out," Spencer said. "So you're safe."

"Wonderful." Charlie relaxed. He could handle nursing Nathan through the rest of his injury now that he knew the assailants were in custody. He held up his free hand. "Why are you referring to Nathan as Sir?"

"That's the third point. I've checked the decree and gone over it with the royal lawyers. You've fulfilled the decree and there's no way Lender could have a claim to the crown. I've also learned that when a man in Nathan's position marries into the royal family, he becomes a Sir. Because you're the king, he's Sir Nathan. He's officially got a title, and once the jubilee happens to commemorate your being fully crowned, he'll be formally recognized as a member of the royal family." Spencer beamed. "So you're not only crowned, but legal, official and blessed."

"We are." Charlie closed his eyes and thanked every last lucky star that he'd succeeded in his ultimate goal of finding love. Sure, he'd managed to secure the crown as well, but as he'd told Nathan, without love, the crown wasn't important. "Spencer?"

"My king?" Spencer tucked the tablet under his arm. "How may I help you?"

"We need to have a crown fashioned for Nathan." If Nathan was healed enough to be presented at the Christmas Eve ball, then he should have a proper crown. "Can you manage that?"

"Of course." Spencer bowed. "I'll work on that now. Do you need anything else from me?"

"No. Thank you." He waited for Spencer to leave, then turned his attention back to Nathan. "I know you won't be at one hundred percent by the ball, but I do wish for you to be present. We should celebrate with the country. As for the big formal wedding...it can wait. You being healthy is more important."

"We'll see what the doctor says, but I can't imagine I wouldn't be permitted to attend the ball. I might not be able to dance with you, but that's okay. I can't dance well." Nathan sighed. "It aches."

"I bet." Charlie gazed at the man he loved. "I have to run the country and there will be plenty of days I won't be home until late. There will be times when I'll have to go abroad as well. I can't guarantee there won't be moments of peril and that things will be smooth sailing for us. The one thing I can guarantee is that you have my heart. I'm devoted to you and River just as much as I am the country. Still think you want to be married to me? Even after all this?"

"I have no doubts." Nathan settled against the pillows. "I knew what I was getting into and I knew this would be hard, but I have no regrets. I'm your partner. River and I love you very much."

Sweeter words hadn't been spoken. "I'd like to adopt River. May I?"

"You want to officially be his father, too?" Nathan smiled. "I can't see why not. We'd be honored for you to be not only his king, but his father."

Charlie let go of Nathan's hand and left the bed long enough stretch out beside him. "I might be a bit too eager as a nurse. I've never had to care for someone this way before."

"I don't mind being a guinea pig." Nathan settled against him. "I'll be fine because you're here."

Charlie closed his eyes and held tight to the man he loved. Life could be funny. One moment, he'd thought he was neck-deep in trouble trying to figure out how to keep the crown. The next, a wonderful man had showed up and made things better. Nathan was truly the best thing to happen to him. The situation might have been a royal mess to start, but with Nathan beside him, everything had turned out just fine.

Chapter Sixteen

Nathan sat on the platform at the Christmas Eve party for the kingdom and stared at the dancers in the crowd. He hadn't expected to be here after the shooting. Some days his muscles still ached, but he grew stronger every day. He appreciated Charlie's attention, too. For being a king, he'd spent plenty of time with Nathan. They felt like a true couple and family now. He'd even had extra time with River. He loved being able to watch him grow, change and start talking more.

Part of him wished River could be at the ball for a longer period of time, but the poor kid hadn't lasted beyond nine that evening, and it was already eleven. If he wasn't careful, Nathan would fall asleep on the platform, too.

He watched the dancers and almost wished he could be out there with them. He wasn't good at dancing and looked more awkward than anything, but he tried. He adjusted the crown, unused to wearing something so heavy on his head. He wasn't important enough to have a crown. Hell, all he'd done was marry the king.

A woman walked up to the platform. Nathan knew her right away and smiled. "Madeline." He left his seat and eased down the steps. "You're here. I wasn't sure if you'd make it."

She bowed. "I wanted to see how River's doing, and when I got the invitation from the king, I couldn't turn it down. I know I was just a vessel for River, but I like the little bugger. He's growing up well."

"Sure is."

"And he'll be a prince?" she asked.

"It's being chewed over." He'd known he'd have to face the surrogate eventually and discuss such matters. She was a sweet woman, and kind, which made talking about River's future easier. She hadn't pushed into their life and expected to parent River, which Nathan appreciated. "How are you?"

"Good. I knew when I saw the rumors of you and the king being together that River would be well cared for." She clasped his hand in hers. "I'd still like to know him when he's old enough to understand what happened. He's a lucky boy to have two dads who love him."

"And a Miss Madeline who loves him, too." He embraced her. "Once he can comprehend what's happened, we'll let him decide what he wants to do."

"Thank you." She stepped back. "How are you feeling? When I heard you'd been shot, I got scared. I've never tried raising a baby and have no idea how. I worried you'd expect me to take care of River. I would, but I wouldn't be as skilled at it as you are."

"I wasn't sure what I'd do," he said. "But I should tell you Charlie wants to adopt River. I'd love it if he could. We're supposed to see the lawyers after the first of the year. I wanted to tell you before we did, but I wasn't sure how. This wasn't the means I wanted to do it, though."

"I'm glad you told me, no matter how you managed it. I encourage him to adopt River." She hugged him again. "I'm going home. It's been a fantastic but long evening. I look forward to the official wedding."

"It's sort of happened—hence this crown." He leaned on the railing. "But the ceremonial wedding will be held on New Year's Day now. With the shooting, we decided to move it from tonight until then."

"Makes a great deal of sense." She slid her palm over his cheek. "Take care of yourself and keep me in the loop. Have a wonderful Christmas."

"You, too." He should have Charlie come over and meet her. Unfortunately, Charlie had his back to Nathan and wasn't turning around. "Good evening, Madeline, and Merry Christmas."

Nathan watched her leave, then settled on the steps to the platform. He'd never been this worn out in his life. The doctor said it might be a bit harder to bounce back after the shooting, and he believed him.

Charlie strolled up to him. "Are you okay?"

"Just tired." He should get up. "Is it so bad that I'm sitting here?" He probably shouldn't be on the steps.

"Nope." Charlie plopped down beside him. "I would like one last dance with you, though. The orchestra will be playing something slow in a moment."

"I'd like that." He stood and held out his hand. "Will you dance with me?"

"Of course." Charlie leapt to his feet and embraced Nathan. "Are you having fun?"

"Mostly." He swayed with the king. "This is a grand celebration, and I love how you've included everyone, but it's taxing."

"The idea was to have this for the kingdom, but we did include a lot of extra security and people." Charlie nuzzled Nathan's nose. "It's a lot to take in and I'm honored you allowed me to be your husband. I'm honored you didn't back out, too. I've done my best to make you happy."

"You have." He loved Charlie more than ever. "You're a good nurse, too."

"I try." He rubbed Nathan's back. "You're just tired?"

"That and I'm hesitant to ask when we can leave." Normally, he'd be perfectly happy to stay up most of the night. "I'd like to see River again before we call it a night, and it's just been a long day."

"Then we can go whenever. It's Christmas Eve and I'd like to spend tonight in our bed." Charlie kept swaying with him. "Let me tell Father we're leaving."

"Okay." He held Charlie's hand as they returned to the platform. King Martin sat with Carrie on the royal chairs—no thrones for anyone, per Charlie's request.

Charlie spoke directly to the king, then left the platform. "Let's go."

Nathan waved to the king before he allowed Charlie to escort him from the grand ballroom.

"I saw you talking to that lady," Charlie said. "She's pretty."

"She's River's surrogate."

Charlie stopped in his tracks. "She is?"

"I tried to get your attention, but you never looked my direction. I'd like you to meet her," Nathan said. "I told her you'd like to adopt River."

"And?" Charlie tensed. "Is she putting up a fight?"

"She encouraged you to do it. She believes you're good for River." Nathan squeezed Charlie's fingers. "It's all okay."

"You have no idea how happy that makes me." Charlie sighed. "That's what I wanted for Christmas."

"It is?" He started walking again with Charlie.

"I wanted our family to be complete and for the barriers to adopting River to go away. Now I'll have my best Christmas because I have the both of you."

"So will I." Being in the castle with River and Charlie was better than he could've ever dreamed. He melted against Charlie. "It's Christmas Eve and I haven't had a chance to get you a proper gift, but I'd like to show my gratitude."

"For?" Charlie kept walking.

"Treating me with dignity and being my support. I love you, Charlie."

"I love you, too." Charlie opened the door to the royal suite. "When you were hurt, I thought I'd lose you, and I vowed not to let anything harm you or River...ever."

"I trust you." Nathan left Charlie long enough to check on River, then joined him in the royal bedroom. He still couldn't get over the enormity of the room. It was big enough for a whole army of people, not just one couple.

Charlie shrugged out of his tuxedo jacket. "Let me help you undress."

"I can do it." He took his coat off. "I'm hurt, but I'm not dying."

"I know." Charlie unbuttoned Nathan's vest and removed his necktie. He lifted the simple crown from Nathan's head. "Do you mind being Sir Nathan?"

"It's odd, but I'll get used to it." He opened his vest and dress shirt. Nathan sat on the bed and toed out of his shoes. "I wish I could've danced and mingled more."

"You're recuperating and it's okay." Charlie ditched his vest, shirt and shoes. "Stretch out. I want you naked."

"You do?" He allowed Charlie to strip him the rest of the way. He didn't have the bandages any longer, but couldn't help being self-conscious about the healing wounds.

"Don't hide from me." Charlie removed the rest of his clothes. He stretched out beside Nathan. "Merry Christmas, my darling."

"Merry Christmas." He tangled up with Charlie. He'd never get tired of kissing him. Charlie tasted like sin and sex, plus he looked hot, too. He caressed Charlie's body and his cock thrummed against Charlie's dick. Excitement rocked through his veins.

He kissed and touched Charlie, loving the feel of his body under his palms. He slid his hands down Charlie's body to his cock. The heat on Charlie's skin and the thrill of touching him added to Nathan's delight. He gathered Charlie's dick and his own in his fingers.

"Oh fuck." Charlie rocked into Nathan's hand. "Are you sure you're up to this?"

He shouldn't be having sex, but that didn't mean he couldn't stroke them both to orgasm. He wanted to make Charlie come apart.

Charlie bit Nathan's bottom lip, then kissed along Nathan's chin to his throat. He grinded in Nathan's hand.

Megan Slayer

A shiver shot down Nathan's spine and he groaned. He fondled then pinched Charlie's nipple. The move elicited a groan from Charlie.

"Nathan." Charlie feathered his lips over Nathan's throat. "You're making me crazy."

The declaration spurred Nathan on. He stroked faster, ratcheting up his own need. Sizzles overwhelmed his body. Every nerve ending was on high alert. Nathan groaned again and met Charlie's gaze. In the light of the moon and the twinkle lights on the tree in the corner, hunger filled Charlie's eyes.

Nathan added pressure and intensity to his strokes. His thoughts blurred and he couldn't breathe. Everything focused on Charlie and how Charlie made him feel.

Charlie shuddered. "Oh, God." His moves turned feral. "Fuck." He jerked in Nathan's hand and cum slid over Nathan's fingers. Nathan added extra strokes to bring on his own orgasm.

Nathan moaned. Seeing and experiencing Charlie's orgasm kickstarted his own. He couldn't hold back. He came on his hand and his belly. Charlie had worn him out from head to toe. His limbs seemed boneless and he slumped on the bed.

Charlie stayed on his side and panted. No words were spoken and Nathan basked in the blessed silence. It gave him time to catch his breath and enjoy the moment. He had a husband and family. He'd gotten everything he'd ever wanted for Christmas and in life. No, he had more.

Nathan settled on his back and stared at the ceiling.

After a few moments, Charlie left the bed long enough to clean them up. When he returned, the

211

mattress dipped. Charlie dragged the blankets over them.

"I never thought I'd find you." Charlie draped his arm across Nathan's belly, careful not to come close to the healing wound. "Never thought we'd have this moment."

"No?" He'd had a strange feeling from the moment he saw Charlie that they'd end up together. Then again, he hadn't thought Charlie was a king, either.

Charlie kissed him. "Thank you for making this rogue royal the man I was always meant to be. Thank you for helping me survive the decree mess and see the truth—I love you and always needed you."

"You're welcome." He closed his eyes. "Love you, Charlie." He hadn't considered Charlie a rogue royal. More like a man on a mission, who happened to have a crown, too. Still, the name 'rogue royal' fit him perfectly. Charlie did things his own way while fulfilling the job of king—and finding a husband. Now the decree and time constraints didn't matter. He and Charlie were the fairy tale come to life. They were meant to be.

Now they would be roguish together.

Want to see more from this author?
Here's a taster for you to enjoy!

Love Me Do:
Loving Summer Rain
Megan Slayer

Coming January 2022

Excerpt

Arthur Burton stepped away from the printer and up to his computer. He'd been told using the standing desk was better for his figure. Standing all day wasn't fun and by the end of his shift, all he wanted to do was sit down. *Oh well. All in a day's work, right?* He'd completed his workout before he'd arrived at the office, so at least he'd burned off calories.

He stared at the notification on his computer. *One new review.* Despite his better judgment to delete the notification, he looked. He prided himself on doing good business and being the best insurance salesman in Norville. He groaned. This review wasn't positive. The wording was downright negative and mean. He cringed — he wanted to do right for people who came to his office.

A dull throb started behind his eyes. He sold insurance for a living, which made him the butt of jokes in the dating world. For some reason, guys didn't see him as a sexy man. They saw him as trying to sell them something. He might have been a personable man, but he was lonely. He'd dated a few times and thought he'd found love in college, but no. Kevin wasn't in it for the long-term. Kevin wanted to play around and hadn't loved Arthur in return. He'd also said Arthur should go by his middle name, Lee. Why? He liked his first name.

He'd been told he was too sensitive. He cared too much about what others said and having the correct appearance. The business was his livelihood. If he didn't keep it going and thriving, then he'd lose everything he'd worked for.

"Boss." Kathy, his secretary and one of his few friends, rested her knuckles on his desk. "Wow. Okay. First, you need to close that tab. You're not going to please everyone. Second, I remember the person who wrote that review."

"She claims I didn't pay attention to her. I didn't correctly create her quote." He rubbed his forehead. "I think I remember her, too. It was for a truck she wanted covered that she owed money on. She wanted minimum coverage and we can't offer that if she has a loan on it."

"Right." She closed the tab on his computer. "She's upset over something we can't change."

"Maybe." One bad review wouldn't kill his business, but he didn't want any negativity like this. He strove to fix all problems and make them right. He couldn't fix this. He sighed. "I'm sorry. You're right. I need to let this go." He needed to remember not everyone would be happy.

"I know you try to make everyone happy and most of the time, it works. You're a good man and you work hard, but some people can't be placated. Besides, you're going to give yourself an ulcer." She leaned forward and stared at him. "You also seem to have forgotten you've got an appointment at Dye Hard Style in half an hour."

"I do?" She was right—he didn't remember the appointment. "In thirty minutes?"

"Yes." She stood tall. "And it sounds like you need to have a chat with James."

"Why?" Normally, his secretary didn't get this involved in his life, but she did care about him, so he should listen to her. "What do you think?"

"You need to get laid." She shrugged. "You need to see James to have him work his magic on your hair and your love life. I also believe you need to relax. You keep yourself so buttoned-up and proper—so much that you'll make yourself sick. Stop doing that."

"I need to stay business-like."

"I know." She rested her hands on her hips. "But there's a difference between being professional and being an automaton. You have so much personality and you hide it. You don't even wear crazy socks or ties. Doesn't bland blue and brown get boring?"

Yes. "No." He groaned. "People expect me to be a certain way. I can't get silly."

She rolled her eyes. "There's silly and there's ridiculous. You've never been ridiculous. That said, wearing argyle socks or a patterned tie won't make you look silly."

"I'll think about what you've just said." He rounded his desk. He wanted to say more, but he wasn't sure how. She'd made her point—a good one, too. "I'll head over to Dye Hard. Thanks."

"Good." She sighed. "I'll prod you toward the right direction, but you need to get moving."

"Thanks." He needed all the help he could get. He watched her leave his office. If he were into women, he might have tried to make a play for her. But he wasn't. He preferred men. The tattooed, purple-haired woman didn't fit into his visual ideal of a secretary, but Kathy did her job well. Despite her ink, piercings and wild-colored hair, she managed to look professional. He admired her freedom and confidence. She looked happy and didn't seem to care what others thought. He needed more of that confidence in his life.

He ensured he had his keys, wallet and phone tucked into his suit coat, then turned his computer screen off. "Kath?"

"Yes, sir?" She appeared in his doorway. "What's up?"

"I'm going over to the salon. Maybe James is running ahead."

She snorted. "That's not going to happen, but you know that and should still get moving. The fresh air on the walk will do you good. Might even help you clear your mind."

"You're right." He glanced back at his desk, then left his office. "I'll return as soon as I can."

"I'll hold down the fort." She clapped him on the shoulder. "I've got this."

"I know you do." He trusted her more than she knew. If she were licensed, he'd make her his co-agent. "I'll be back."

"See you." She waved. "Come back sexy."

He laughed. "I doubt that'll happen." But he could let James try. He left the office and walked the three blocks to Dye Hard Style.

Along the way, he drank in the views of Norville. His hometown wasn't a big one. Norville had a state-of-the-art softball complex for the girls' softball teams, wonderful parks and a pretty circle in the center of town, but not much else. The townsfolk alternatively loved and hated the roundabout. The statue at the center of the circle was supposed to be the image of the town founder, Clarence Norville, but the nose had long broken off and one arm had been damaged in a windstorm. People claimed the statue was the spirit of Norville, rather than any one person.

Spirit aside, nothing much happened in Norville. The festivals were long gone and people tended to gather for the yearly softball tournaments and football seasons. The girls' softball team dominated each year, often winning at the state events. The high school football team wasn't so hot, but the players tried and the town was dedicated to the sport.

The one thing the town did have going for it was the architecture. Almost all the buildings along the main drag were over a hundred years old, looked their age, but still managed to be structurally sound and beautiful. All had ornate carving in the brickwork and names embedded at the apex of each. Many featured stone entryways and flower boxes that the business owners lovingly kept full of blossoms all spring and summer. Arthur worked hard to make his storefront shine along with the rest.

The one building that stuck out was the old movie theater. Movies hadn't been shown there in years, but the neon and chrome on the building still glimmered. The neon was the signature look for the salon that had taken over the building. The concession stand served as the counter for buying hair care products and scheduling appointments. The rest of the room belonged to the styling stations. The auditorium had been turned into an event hall for weddings and social gatherings. He admired the owner's decision to keep the original façade for the building and worked with the spirit of the space, rather than changing it. The modifications ensured the building was used and appreciated. No one knew the owner, though. If he'd come to the chamber of commerce meetings, Arthur had never seen him.

Everyone in town knew to visit Dye Hard Style. James, the head stylist, did wonders with all sorts of hair. He also knew how to couple people up.

Arthur opened the door to the salon. A scruffy dog trotted in beside him and strode right past the scheduling station. Arthur frowned. Did the dog belong to the owner or James?

"Hi." Clarke, the receptionist, beckoned from the ticket counter. "Did you bring your pup along? He's rough around the edges, but cute."

"He's not mine. I don't know him." He stopped at the counter. "I have an appointment."

"Arthur." Clarke grinned. "James is ready for you."

"He is?" He was early.

"He is." Clarke frowned and opened the gate. The dog trotted in first and made himself comfortable strolling along the styling stations. Clarke snorted. "Looks like the dog wants a style, too."

"I guess so. Maybe James knows him." He ventured over to James' chair.

James knelt in front of the dog. "You're back."

"I just got here." Arthur petted the dog. "Or do you mean him?"

"Him." James scratched the dog behind the ears. "He's shown up every day this week. No tags, no collar. I even asked around and no one has ever seen him before."

"Maybe he's adopted you." Arthur folded his arms. "He might have. Do you want a dog?"

"I never thought about it." James stood and retrieved a bowl. "I've fed him and he gets water." He filled the bowl with water. "Let me finish here and wash my hands."

"I bet he adopted you."

"I think you're right." James gestured to the chair. "Now, you're here for a cut and style." He washed his hands. "Sit. Do you know what you want? Any ideas for your style? Tell me your troubles. Remember, I'm like Vegas. What's told to the stylist stays with the stylist."

Arthur took his place in the chair and waited until he'd donned the cape. "I need to think about anything but the semi-crappy day I'm having."

"Then let's polish you, beautiful." James turned the chair around and tipped it back. "What happened, doll? Why is your day semi-crappy?" He turned on the water, wetting Arthur's hair.

"It's silly really." He loved when someone washed his hair. The act relaxed him. He bit back a sigh as James shampooed him. "I got a bad review and I let it get me down."

"Oh, honey. We get the odd bad reviews, too. You can't make everyone happy." James rinsed Arthur's hair. "They get a color they begged for but don't want, or say they want everything cut off then change their mind after the haircut. I can work miracles, but not every one of them will be miraculous."

"I get it."

James sat him up and covered his head with a towel. "So, forget the review, honey. Focus on what you can change."

"I'll keep doing my job, then." That sounded easy enough.

"Then there you go." James turned him around to face the mirror. "So, what are we doing?"

"A trim and polish. Just neaten me up." His heart sank. He was too buttoned-up already and not getting out of his comfort zone wasn't helping much.

James stared at him through the reflection in the mirror. "May I try something? It won't be too drastic, but I want to try a slightly different look for you."

James had the ability to style individuals to make their uniqueness shine. If he had an idea for Arthur, who was he to argue? "Okay."

"Yeah?" James grinned. The piercing in his bottom lip sparkled. "You're sure?"

"I am." He needed something. This could be the small change required.

"Good." James combed Arthur's wet hair. "Why do you look so lonely and sad, doll? Not because of that review? Talk to me."

He kept so much bottled up. If he couldn't tell his stylist, who could he tell? "Because I am lonely."

"Why? You're handsome, have your own business, are smart..." James parted Arthur's hair, then began trimming. "What's not to like about you?"

"I don't know, but I don't give myself the chance to look for guys, that's one thing." He cringed. "That sounds doofy."

"No, you sound scared and like you need a little help." James continued cutting. "You need a matchmaker."

"I do." He shouldn't have admitted that out loud, but oh well.

"What do you want in a guy?" James asked.

He sighed, buying himself some time to think. "I want a man who is kind, considerate, who will work with me and make me better. A partner. I want a guy who isn't afraid to date an insurance agent. Someone who sees beyond the shell and won't let me get complacent."

"And looks?" James stared at their reflection. He narrowed his eyes, then resumed cutting. "You must have a type."

"Not really. I like guys based on their attitude and ability to empathize. It's about being drawn to the man," Arthur said. "You know? If there's a spark when we're talking, then that's the thing. If there isn't, then I don't bother."

"I do." James finished cutting, then combed Arthur's hair. "Sometimes, you just know the guy is right."

"Yes." That was it exactly.

James stopped touching Arthur. "Well...try this." He turned Arthur away from the mirror, then finger-combed Arthur's hair. "Okay, this." He swiveled Arthur back to face the mirror. "Well?"

Arthur stared at himself. He looked like him, but the haircut with his part on the left looked more correct. It accentuated his eyes and appeared professional. "That's awesome."

"Yeah?" James plunged the comb into the blue solution and his scissors into the sink. He wiped his hands. "About your dating situation...go to Club Jester on Friday at nine. Dress like you, but be casual. I want you to meet my friend, Summer Rain."

"A girl?" He'd never heard of anyone named Summer Rain.

"No, he's a guy." James removed the cape. "A great guy who ticks your boxes."

"Named Summer Rain?" It seemed like an odd moniker for a man.

"Yes, and trust me. I have the golden touch." James picked up a tablet. "Do you want a two-month appointment or six weeks?"

"Six weeks." He set up his next slot with James, then offered his credit card to pay. "You said nine on Friday night?"

"Yes. Club Jester. His name is Summer Rain. It'll be great." James swiped the card. "If you don't hit it off, then the next appointment is on me."

He had nothing to lose. "Okay."

"You'll be meeting your destiny." James handed him back the card. "Plus, you look fierce. Any man would be nuts to pass you up."

He wasn't sure he believed James, but why not? "You're right."

"I know I am." James winked. "Feel better?"

"I do." Almost like he could conquer the world. He handed James a twenty as a tip.

"Then there we go. Thank you and I'll see you in six weeks." James grinned. "Maybe I'll have named the dog by then."

"I'll bet you do." Maybe he'd find love by then, too. It couldn't hurt to try.

About the Author

Megan Slayer, aka Wendi Zwaduk, is a multi-published, award-winning author of more than one-hundred short stories and novels. She's been writing since 2008 and published since 2009. Her stories range from the contemporary and paranormal to LGBTQ and BDSM themes. No matter what the length, her works are always hot, but with a lot of heart. She enjoys giving her characters a second chance at love, no matter what the form. She's been the runner up in the Kink Category at Love Romances Café as well as nominated at the LRC for best author, best contemporary, best ménage and best anthology. Her books have made it to the bestseller lists on Amazon.com.

When she's not writing, Megan spends time with her husband and son as well as three dogs and three cats. She enjoys art, music and racing, but football is her sport of choice.

Megan loves to hear from readers. You can find her contact information, website details and author profile page at https://www.pride-publishing.com

PUBLISHING

Sign up for our newsletter and find out about all our romance book releases, eBook sales and promotions, sneak peeks and FREE romance books!